TH

Siegfried's Murder

TRANSLATED BY A. T. HATTO

PENGUIN EPICS

PENGUIN BOOKS

Published by the Penguin Group
Penguin Books Ltd, 80 Strand, London WC2R ORL, England
Penguin Group (USA) Inc., 375 Hudson Street, New York, New York 10014, USA
Penguin Group (Canada), 90 Eglinton Avenue East, Suite 700, Toronto, Ontario, Canada M4P 2Y3
(a division of Pearson Penguin Canada Inc.)
Penguin Ireland, 25 St Stephen's Green, Dublin 2, Ireland (a division of Penguin Books Ltd)
Penguin Group (Australia), 250 Camberwell Road, Camberwell, Victoria 3124, Australia
(a division of Pearson Australia Group Pty Ltd)
Penguin Books India Pvt Ltd, 11 Community Centre, Panchsheel Park, New Delhi – 110 017, India
Penguin Group (NZ), cnr Airborne and Rosedale Roads, Albany,
Auckland 1310, New Zealand (a division of Pearson New Zealand Ltd)
Penguin Books (South Africa) (Pty) Ltd, 24 Sturdee Avenue,
Rosebank, Johannesburg 2196, South Africa

Penguin Books Ltd, Registered Offices: 80 Strand, London WC2R ORL, England

www.penguin.com

This translation of *The Nibelungenlied* first published 1965
Reissued with revisions 1969
This extract published in Penguin Books 2006
1

Translation copyright © A. T. Hatto, 1965, 1969
All rights reserved

The moral right of the translator has been asserted

Taken from the Penguin Classics edition of *The Nibelungenlied*, translated by A. T. Hatto

Typeset by Rowland Phototypesetting Ltd, Bury St Edmunds, Suffolk
Printed in England by Clays Ltd, St Ives plc

ISBN-13: 978-0-141-02640-6
ISBN-10: 0-141-02640-5

Contents

Note

This extract is from *The Nibelungenlied*, a powerful story of murder and revenge. Written by an unknown author in the twelfth century, this great epic poem reaches back to the earliest epochs of German antiquity, transforming ancient versions of the tale into a masterpiece.

Kriemhild

We have been told in ancient tales many marvels of famous heroes, of mighty toil, joys, and high festivities, of weeping and wailing, and the fighting of bold warriors – of such things you can now hear wonders unending!

In the land of the Burgundians there grew up a maiden of high lineage, so fair that none in any land could be fairer. Her name was Kriemhild. She came to be a beautiful woman, causing many knights to lose their lives. This charming girl was as if made for love's caresses: she was desired by brave fighting men and none was her enemy, for her noble person was beyond all measure lovely. Such graces did the young lady possess that she was the adornment of her sex. She was in the care of three great and noble kings, the renowned warriors Gunther and Gernot, and young Giselher, a splendid knight, and she was sister to these princes who had the charge of her. These lords were of high race, magnanimous, strong, and brave beyond measure, altogether rare warriors. Their country was called Burgundy, and in days to come they wrought mighty wonders in Etzel's land. They held sway at Worms beside the Rhine, and were served in high honour by many proud knights from their territories till their dying day, when the enmity of two noble ladies was to bring them to a sad end. The great queen their mother was named Uote, and their father, who had bequeathed them their heritage, was called Dancrat. A man of abounding valour, Dancrat too had won great fame in younger days. These three kings, as I have said, were of high courage and they also had as their vassals the best warriors whose deeds were ever told, strong, brave, and resolute in sharp encounters, Hagen of Troneck and his valiant brother Dancwart, Ortwin of Metz, the two margraves Gere and Eckewart, and Volker of Alzei, a man of flawless courage. Rumold, who was Lord of the Kitchen and an excellent knight, and lords Sindold and Hunold, all vassals of the three kings, were charged with maintaining their court and their renown, and they had many other men besides whom I cannot name. Dancwart was Marshal, his nephew Ortwin was the King's Seneschal, Sindold was Cup-bearer – he was a splendid knight – and Hunold was Chamberlain. These were well able to maintain the court's high honour, and indeed none could recount to the full its power and far-flung dominion, or the glory and chivalry those lords rejoiced in all their lives.

Living in such magnificence, Kriemhild dreamt she reared a falcon, strong, handsome and wild, but that two eagles rent it while she perforce looked on, the most grievous thing that could ever befall her. She told her dream to her mother Uote, who could give the good maiden no better reading than this: 'The falcon you are rearing is a noble man who, unless God preserve him, will soon be taken from you.'

'Why do you talk to me of a man, dear Mother? I

intend to stay free of a warrior's love all my life. I mean to keep my beauty till I die, and never be made wretched by the love of any man.'

'Do not forswear it too firmly,' rejoined her mother. 'If you are ever to know heartfelt happiness it can come only from a man's love. If God should assign to you a truly worthy knight you will grow to be a beautiful woman.'

'Let us speak of other things, my lady. There are many examples of women who have paid for happiness with sorrow in the end. I shall avoid both, and so I shall come to no harm.'

Kriemhild set all thought of love aside, and after this conversation the good girl passed many a pleasant day unaware of any man whom she would love. Yet the time came when she was wed with honour to a very brave warrior, to that same falcon whom she had seen in the dream which her mother had interpreted for her. What terrible vengeance she took on her nearest kinsmen for slaying him in days to come! For his one life there died many a mother's child.

2
Siegfried

Down the Rhine, in the splendid, far-famed city of Xanten in the Netherlands, there grew up a royal prince, a gallant knight named Siegfried, son of Siegmund and Sieglind. Fired by his courage, he tried the mettle of many kingdoms and rode through many lands to put his strength to the test. Later, in Burgundy, he was to meet a host of valiant knights. Of his best days, when he was young, marvels could be told of the honours that accrued to him and of his handsome looks, so that women of great beauty came to love him. He was reared with all the care that befitted his high station, and acquired many fine qualities of his own. It gave lustre to his father's kingdom that he was found altogether so distinguished. He had now grown up sufficiently to ride to court, where many were glad to see him. Indeed many ladies, both married and maidens, hoped he would always wish to come there; for (as lord Siegfried was aware) no few were well-disposed towards him.

The young man was never allowed to go riding without escort. By Siegmund's and Sieglind's command he was dressed in elegant clothes, and experienced men well-versed in matters of honour had him in their charge, as a result of which he was able to win all hearts. He had grown to be strong enough to bear arms expertly, and he possessed in abundance all the needful qualities. As to the lovely women he wooed, he showed discernment, and they for their part would have done themselves high honour in loving fearless Siegfried.

When the time was ripe, his father Siegmund had it made known to his vassals that he wished to hold a festivity in company with his dear friends, and the news was borne to other kingdoms. The King bestowed horses and fine clothes on native and stranger alike. And wherever there were noble squires of his line of an age to be knighted, they were invited to his country to take part in the festivity; and when the time came they received their swords in company with the prince.

It was a magnificent feast, and well did Siegmund and Sieglind know how to win esteem with the lavish gifts they made, so that many people from other parts came riding to their country. Four hundred knights-aspirant were to be attired with Siegfried: thus many comely young ladies, wishing him well, toiled busily, setting in gold brocade jewel upon jewel, which, as custom required, they planned to work with silk-and-gold trimmings into the proud young warriors' clothes.

Then, at midsummer, when his son was knighted, the King commanded seats to be set for the valiant company, whereupon a host of noble squires and knights of high rank repaired to the minster. The older men did well to wait upon the novices as they had been waited upon at their own knighting; it passed the time agreeably for them, and they had hope of pleasures to come. Mass was sung to the glory of God, and at once there was a great press where, in accordance with chivalric custom, the squires were to be knighted amid such splendour as can scarcely be seen again.

They ran to where many chargers stood saddled, and the bohort in Siegmund's courtyard grew so tremendous that the palace thundered with the din which those spirited warriors made, while you could hear thrust on thrust by young and old, so that the shivering of shafts rang loud on the air and you could see all these knights send the splinters flying far and wide before the hall – so zestfully did they set to.

Their host asked them to make an end, and their mounts were led away. You could see many strong bosses all broken, and precious stones that had been torn from gleaming shield-plates and strewn upon the grass, the work of mighty lance-thrusts.

Then the King's guests went and sat where they were bidden. The profusion of rare dishes and the excellent wine that were set before them in great abundance banished their fatigue – all honour was paid to both friends and strangers. And although they well amused themselves the livelong day, there were many strolling entertainers who, in their eagerness to earn the rich gifts to be had there, put all thought of rest aside, so that Siegmund's whole kingdom was gilded by their praises. And now the King commanded young Siegfried to bestow lands and castles in fee, as he himself had done when he was knighted, and Siegfried enfeoffed his companions richly, so that they were well pleased with their journey there.

The celebrations had lasted for a week when, in

honour of her son, Sieglind dispensed gifts of red gold, in accordance with ancient custom, for she well knew how to win the people's favour for him. No wandering minstrel remained poor there – it rained horses and clothes as though their donors had not a day to live! I cannot imagine that any royal household ever practised such munificence.

Those who had come to the festivity dispersed in grand style. Powerful nobles were afterwards heard to say that they would gladly have the young man for their lord: but handsome Siegfried did not want it, Siegmund's and Sieglind's beloved son did not wish to wear the crown so long as both were alive; yet as a valiant knight he aspired to dominion that he might ward off all the violence which he feared for his country.

3

How Siegfried came to Worms

This prince was never troubled by heartfelt sorrow. But one day he heard a report that there was a maiden living in Burgundy who was of perfect beauty; and from her, as it fell out, he was to receive much joy, yet also great distress.

The young lady's most rare beauty was known far and wide, and many warriors had also learned of her spirited disposition, so that her perfections attracted many visitors to Gunther's country. But however many suitors came to woo her, Kriemhild never admitted to herself in her inmost thoughts that she wanted any as her lover, since as yet her future lord was a stranger to her.

Siegfried's thoughts were now bent on a noble attachment, and beside his claims to favour all others were as nothing. Brave Siegfried was well endowed to win the hearts of lovely women, and in the event noble Kriemhild became his wife.

Seeing that he aspired to a constant love, his kinsmen and many of his vassals counselled him to woo a lady of suitable standing. 'I shall take Kriemhild the fair maiden of Burgundy,' he answered boldly, 'on account of her very great beauty, since even if the mightiest of emperors wished to marry, I know he would not demean himself in loving the noble princess.'

The affair came to Siegmund's ears through the gossip of his courtiers, who said that Siegfried meant to woo the noble maiden, a design which grieved his father deeply. Queen Sieglind learned of this too, and, having no illusions about Gunther and his men, she feared greatly for the life of her son. Thus they tried to turn the young knight's thoughts against this enterprise.

'But, dear father,' answered Siegfried, 'rather than not woo where my heart finds great delight, I would quite forgo the love of noble ladies. All would be in vain, whatever anyone should say.'

'If you are set on it, then I am heartily glad of your intentions,' replied the King, 'and I shall help you to accomplish them to the best of my powers. Yet, remember, Gunther has many proud vassals. Were there no other than Hagen, he has such haughty ways that I fear we might regret it if we asked for the Princess's hand.'

'How should that trouble us?' asked Siegfried. 'Whatever I fail to get from them by friendly requests, I shall take by my own valour. I fancy I shall wrest their lands and people from them.'

'What you say distresses me,' replied King Siegmund, 'since if this were repeated at Worms they would never let you ride into Burgundy. I have known Gunther's and Gernot's ways for a long time now. I have been told on good authority that none will ever win the girl by force. But if you mean to ride there in the company of warriors I shall put our friends to the test and summon them at once.'

'It is not my wish and indeed I should regret it if warriors were to accompany me to Burgundy on a warlike expedition to win the handsome girl, for I am well able to gain her by my own unaided powers. I shall go to Gunther's country as one of a band of twelve, and you must help me to get there, father.' Following this his stalwarts were furnished with clothes lined with vari-coloured squirrel.

This came to the ears of his mother Sieglind, too. Fearing to lose him at the hands of Gunther's vassals, the noble Queen shed many tears in sad concern for her darling son. But lord Siegfried went to see her and, addressing her kindly, said: 'You must not weep for me, my lady. I shall not go in fear of any fighting-man, I promise you. And if you will help me on my march to Burgundy by providing me and my followers with clothes such as proud warriors may wear with honour, I shall thank you most sincerely.'

'Since you will not be dissuaded,' answered the lady Sieglind, 'I will help you on your journey, though you are my only son, and I shall give you and your companions to take with you ample stocks of the finest clothes that knights ever wore.'

Young Siegfried thanked the Queen with a bow. 'I intend to have on my journey twelve warriors all told,' he said, 'and it is for them that the clothes must be made. I should much like to see how matters stand with Kriemhild.'

Thus lovely women sat day and night with scarcely any rest till Siegfried's clothes were ready, since he was firmly resolved on his journey. His father commanded the knightly equipment in which Siegfried was going abroad to be richly adorned, while gleaming corselets, sturdy helmets, and fine broad shields were made ready for his companions.

When the time drew near for them to set out for Burgundy, people began anxiously to wonder whether they would ever return; but the warriors themselves ordered their clothes and armour to be loaded on to pack-horses. Their chargers were handsome and their harness shone red with gold; and if there were any men alive who were prouder than Siegfried and his companions, they had no cause to be so. Siegfried now asked leave to depart for Burgundy, and the King and Queen sadly granted it, at which he consoled them affectionately. 'Do not weep on my account,' he said. 'Never fear that I shall ever be in danger.'

The knights were sorry at his going, and many young ladies wept. I imagine their hearts had truly foretold them that it would end in death for so many of their friends. They were lamenting not without reason, they had good cause to do so.

A week later, in the morning, Siegfried's valiant company rode on to the sandy riverbank at Worms. All their equipment shone red with gold, their chargers went with even pace, their harness was good to see; they bore bright new shields of ample width, their helmets were very handsome, and never were such magnificent robes seen upon warriors as when Siegfried rode to court in Gunther's land. The points of their swords dangled beside their spurs, and these excellent knights carried sharp spears – Siegfried's had a head two spans across, with fearful cutting edges. Their hands held golden bridles, and the poitrels were of silk.

In such style did they arrive. Crowds began to stare at them on all sides as many of Gunther's vassals ran out to meet them. Proud warriors, knights and squires alike, they went out to those lords as they were bound to do and they welcomed the strangers to their master's country and relieved them of mounts and shields.

The squires were about to lead the chargers to stable, when brave Siegfried quickly said: 'Leave our horses where they are. We shall soon be riding away, for such is my intention. If anyone knows where I can find the great King Gunther of Burgundy, let him tell me frankly.'

'You can easily find him if you wish,' answered one of their number who knew. 'I saw him with his warriors in that spacious hall. Go there, and you will find him in the company of fine men in plenty.'

Now it was announced to the King that some gay knights had arrived, clad in dazzling corselets and magnificent robes, though none in Burgundy knew them. The King was curious to know where these lordly warriors were from, in their bright clothes and with their fine, broad, new shields, and he was sorry that none could tell him. But Ortwin of Metz, who was accounted both mighty and brave, made answer: 'Since we do not know a man of them, send for my uncle Hagen and let him take a look at them – he knows all the kingdoms and foreign countries – so that if these lords are known to him he will tell us.' The King accordingly summoned Hagen and his men, and as they came to court they made a splendid sight.

Hagen asked the King's pleasure.

'There are strange knights within my walls whom nobody knows. If you have ever seen them, Hagen, tell me who they are.'

'I will do so,' answered Hagen. Going to a window, he directed his gaze to the strangers. Their whole turnout pleased him greatly, but they were total strangers to him here in Burgundy. He declared that wherever these knights had come from to Worms, they must be either princes or princes' envoys, judging by their handsome chargers and splendid clothes, and that whichever land they had left, they were men of spirit.

'Although I have never seen him,' said Hagen, 'I dare assert my belief that the knight who makes such a magnificent figure there is Siegfried, whatever his purpose. He is bringing unheard-of news to this country, for this warrior slew the bold Nibelungs, the two mighty princes Schilbung and Nibelung, and marvellous are the deeds he has done since in his great strength. Riding unaccompanied past the foot of a mountain (as I was truly told), he chanced upon a host of valiant men whom he had never seen before, gathered round Nibelung's treasure, all of which they had borne out from a cavern. Now hear the strange tale how the Nibelungs were intent on dividing it! – Siegfried marvelled as he watched them, for he came so near that he could see those warriors and they him. "Here comes mighty Siegfried of the Netherlands," said one of them; and mysterious were the things which he experienced among them. Siegfried was well received by Schilbung and Nibelung, and these noble young princes begged and implored the handsome man by common consent to make division of the treasure, and this he promised to do. He saw so many precious stones, we are told, that a hundred baggage-waggons could not have carried them, and an even greater quantity of red gold of Nibelung's country; all of which bold Siegfried was asked to divide for them. They gave him Nibelung's sword in payment, but they had scant profit from the service which the good warrior was to render them. He was unable to finish his task, so enraged were they. But although they had twelve brave men among their friends there – mighty giants they were – how could it avail them? Siegfried slew them in a fury and he also subdued seven hundred men of Nibelungland with the good sword Balmung, so that, in dread of this sword and also of brave Siegfried, a host of young warriors yielded the land and its castles to him as their lord. Furthermore he slew the mighty princes Schilbung and Nibelung, and he came in great peril from Alberich who hoped to avenge his masters there and then, till Siegfried's huge strength was brought home to him; for the powerful dwarf was no match for him. They then ran towards the cavern like raging lions, and here he won from Alberich the cloak of invisibility. Thus Siegfried, terrible man, was now lord of all the treasure.

'All who had dared fight lay slain there. Siegfried commanded the hoard to be taken back to the cave whence Nibelung's men had fetched it, and, after swearing oaths to Siegfried that he would be his humble servitor, Alberich was made lord treasurer. Indeed, he was in all ways ready to do his bidding.

'These are the deeds that he has done,' continued

Hagen of Troneck. 'No warrior was ever so strong. But I know more concerning him. This hero slew a dragon and bathed in its blood, from which his skin grew horny so that no weapon will bite it, as has been shown time and time again. We must receive this young lord with more than usual honour, lest we incur his enmity. He is so valiant and has performed so many marvels thanks to his bodily strength that it is best to have his friendship.'

'I am sure you are right,' replied the great King. 'Just see how he stands there all eager for battle, together with his men, the image of a fearless warrior! Let us go down to meet him.'

'You may do so without loss of honour,' said Hagen, 'since he is of noble race, the son of a mighty King. I'll swear from his manner that it is no trifle which brings him riding here.'

'Then he is welcome,' answered the King. 'You have told me that he is both well-born and brave, and he shall profit from it here in Burgundy.' Thus Gunther went out to Siegfried and, accompanied by his warriors, received their visitor with flawless courtesy, so that the handsome man inclined his head in thanks for their fair welcome.

'I should very much like to know where you have come from, noble Siegfried, and what business it is that brings you here to Worms on the Rhine?'

'This I shall not hide from you,' the stranger answered him. 'I was told repeatedly in my father's country that the bravest warriors that King ever had were to be found with you, and I have come to see for myself. I have also heard such warlike qualities ascribed to you that

15

(according to many people in all the lands about) a more valiant prince was never seen; nor shall I desist till I know the truth of it. I, too, am a warrior and am entitled to wear a crown, but I wish to achieve the reputation of possessing a land and people in my own sole right, for which my head and honour shall be pledge! Now since (as they tell me) you are so brave – and I do not care who minds – I will wrest from you by force all that you possess! Your lands and your castles shall all be subject to me!'

The King and his vassals were amazed to hear this news that Siegfried meant to deprive him of his lands, and as Gunther's warriors listened they felt their anger rise.

'But how have I deserved that through the strength of any man we should lose what my father so long maintained in honour?' asked Gunther. 'Were we to let this happen it would be poor proof that we, too, practise the art of war.'

'I shall not yield my claim,' answered the fearless man. 'Unless you can protect your country by your own valour I shall rule the whole of it: but if you can wrest my inheritance from me this shall be subject to you. Now let us stake our patrimonies one against the other, and whichever of us two proves victorious let him be master of both lands and peoples.'

Hagen and Gernot were quick to advise against it. 'We do not aspire to gain any land by force at the price of the slaying of one warrior by another,' answered Gernot. 'We possess rich territories that render service to us as to their rightful lords, nor could they be in better keeping.'

The King's friends stood round him with fierce anger in their hearts, among them Ortwin of Metz. 'These terms displease me greatly,' said he. 'Mighty Siegfried has challenged you without provocation. Even if you and your brothers lacked forces to defend you, and he came at the head of a royal army, I fancy I should compel him with very good reason to have done with such swaggering!'

This stung the warrior from the Netherlands to anger. 'Do not presume to raise your hand against me: I am a mighty King, while you are but a king's vassal. I tell you, a dozen such as you could never face up to me in battle!'

True nephew of Hagen that he was, Ortwin shouted for swords. The King was sorry that Hagen kept silent so long. But Gernot, as brave as he was unabashed, intervened.

'Put your anger by,' he told Ortwin. 'My advice is this. Lord Siegfried has done nothing to us that we cannot settle courteously, so that we may have him for our friend. This would be more to our credit.'

'We, your knights, have every cause to resent his riding here to Worms to battle,' declared mighty Hagen. 'He ought to have refrained. My lords would never have wronged him so.'

'If what I have said irks you, lord Hagen,' retorted Siegfried, the powerful man, 'I will show you that I mean to have the upper hand here in Burgundy.'

'It falls to me to prevent it,' rejoined Gernot. And he forbade all his followers to say anything in arrogance that might arouse Siegfried's displeasure, while Siegfried, too, was mollified by thoughts of lovely Kriemhild.

'Why should we fight you?' asked Gernot. 'For all the warriors that must die we should gain little honour and you small profit from it.'

But Siegfried, son of King Siegmund, answered: 'What are Hagen and Ortwin waiting for, that they and the many friends whom Hagen has here do not rush into the fray?' – But these had to keep their peace as Gernot had commanded them.

'We bid you welcome,' said Uote's son, 'together with your comrades-in-arms who have accompanied you! I and my kinsmen shall be glad to attend you.' Word was given to pour out Gunther's wine in greeting, after which the King declared: 'Everything we have is at your disposal, provided you accept it honourably. Our lives and our wealth shall be shared with you in common.'

Lord Siegfried was somewhat appeased. Orders were given to store their gear away, while the best possible quarters were sought for Siegfried's squires, and they were made very comfortable. In the days that followed, Siegfried was a most welcome guest among the Burgundians, and, believe me, he was honoured by them for his manly courage a thousand times more than I can tell you, so that none could see him and harbour any grudge against him. When the kings and their vassals sought recreation, Siegfried was always the best, whatever they did: he was so strong that none was a match for him, whether at putting the weight or throwing the javelin. And whenever gay knights were passing the time with the ladies and displaying their good breeding, people were glad to see him, for he aspired to a noble love. Whatever the company undertook, Siegfried was ready to join in. Meanwhile he cherished a lovely girl in his heart and was cherished in return by this same young lady whom he had never seen but who in her own intimate circle nevertheless often spoke kindly of him. When the young knights and squires had a mind for some sport in the courtyard, the noble princess Kriemhild would often look on from the window, and as long as it lasted she needed no other entertainment. Had Siegfried but known that his beloved was observing him, it would have been a source of unending delight to him, and if he could have seen her I dare assert no greater pleasure could ever have befallen him. And when he stood in the courtyard among the warriors to pass the time, as people still do today, Sieglind's son made such a handsome figure that many fell deeply in love with him.

As to Siegfried, he often thought: 'How shall it ever come about that I may set eyes on this noble young lady? It saddens me that she whom I love with all my heart and have long so loved, remains an utter stranger to me.'

And whenever the great kings rode on circuit through their lands, their retainers perforce accompanied them and Siegfried among them, much to Kriemhild's regret, while he, too, was often in great distress from the love he bore her.

Thus Siegfried, you must know, lived with those lords in Gunther's land for a year on end without ever having seen the lovely maiden who was to bring him much joy and yet much sorrow, too.

4

How Siegfried fought with the Saxons

Strange tidings were on their way to Gunther's country, borne by envoys that had been sent to the Burgundians from afar by unknown warriors who nevertheless were their enemies; hearing which, Gunther and his men were greatly vexed. I shall name those warriors for you. They were Liudeger, the proud and mighty sovereign of Saxony, and Liudegast, King of Denmark, and they were bringing a host of lordly intruders with them on their campaign.

The messengers whom these enemies of Gunther had sent into his country had arrived, and the strangers were asked their business and at once summoned into the presence of the King, who gave them a friendly greeting. 'You are welcome!' said the good King. 'Now tell us who it was that sent you here, for I have yet to learn it.' But they were much afraid of Gunther's wrath.

'If you will permit us to tell you the message we bring, Sire, we shall not stay silent but shall name you the lords who have sent us. They are Liudegast and Liudeger; and they intend to invade your country. You have provoked their anger and, truly, we were told that these lords bear you great hostility. They mean to launch an expedition against Worms on the Rhine, and you can take my word for it that they have many knights to support them. In twelve weeks from now their campaign will be launched, so that you must soon let it be seen whether you have any staunch friends to help you to guard your lands and castles; for the men of Liudegast and Liudeger will hack many helmets and shields to pieces here. But if you wish to treat with them, send a message to that effect, and then the numerous forces of your mighty enemies will not draw near to do you such harm as must lead to the destruction of countless gallant knights.'

'Now wait a little until I have considered this affair,' answered the good King, 'and then I will tell you my mind. I shall not keep this momentous news from whatever trusty followers I may have; rather shall I complain of it to my friends.'

Mighty Gunther was deeply downcast. He kept the matter privy to his own thoughts, sent for Hagen and others of his men, and summoned Gernot urgently to court. When the noblest that could be found were assembled, he addressed them.

'Our country is threatened with invasion by strong attacking forces. I call on you to support me!'

'Let us ward it off, sword in hand,' answered gallant Gernot. 'They alone die that are doomed. Leave them for the dead men they are. Such things shall not make me forget my honour! Our enemies are welcome!'

'I would not advise that,' said Hagen of Troneck. 'Liudegast and Liudeger are of arrogant temper, and we cannot muster our forces so soon. But,' added the valiant warrior, 'why do you not tell Siegfried?'

Word was given to lodge the envoys in the town, and

whatever the hatred that was felt for them, it was right of mighty Gunther to have them well cared for till he should learn from his friends who was going to stand by him. Yet the King was in great anxiety and distress, and Siegfried, gay young knight, seeing Gunther so downcast, asked him to tell him all about it, since he could not know what had happened to him.

'I am much surprised,' he said, 'that the cheerful demeanour which you have shown us all along is so altered.'

'I cannot tell everyone of the vexations I have to bear, locked away in my heart,' answered handsome Gunther. 'One should complain of one's wrongs to proven friends.'

Siegfried turned pale, and then red. 'I have never denied you anything,' he answered the King. 'I shall help you to avert all your troubles. If you are looking for friends I shall assuredly be one among them, and I trust I shall acquit myself honourably till the end of my days.'

'May God reward you, lord Siegfried, for I like your words. And if your manly courage never comes to my aid I shall nevertheless rejoice that you wish me so well, and if I live for any time you shall be well rewarded. I will tell you why I am downcast. I have been informed by my enemies' envoys that they intend to attack me here, a thing that warriors have never done to us in Burgundy before.'

'Do not let that weigh on you,' said Siegfried, 'but calm your fears. Do as I ask – let me win honour and advantage for you, while you on your part summon your knights to your aid. Even though your powerful enemies had thirty thousand knights to help them and

I only a thousand, I should face them in battle. You can rely on me!'

'I shall always seek to repay you,' replied King Gunther.

'Then muster a thousand of your men for me (since apart from a dozen warriors I have none of my own with me) and I shall defend your lands – for Siegfried will always serve you loyally. Hagen and Ortwin, Dancwart and Sindold, your beloved stalwarts, must help us, and brave Volker must ride with them – indeed Volker must bear your standard, since there is none I would give it to more willingly. As to the envoys, let them ride home to their lords' countries and inform their masters that they shall see us very soon and to such purpose that peace shall be assured for our cities.'

The King summoned his kinsmen and vassals accordingly.

[. . .]

They rode with their warriors from the Rhine through Hesse towards Saxony, where there was fighting later. They laid waste the countryside with fire and pillage, to the great distress of the two kings, when they came to hear of it. Never had the Saxons suffered greater loss from invasion.

[. . .]

The captains of the two kings led their forces on, and Siegfried, too, had arrived with those whom he had brought from the Netherlands. Many a hand was reddened in the blood of battle that day. Sindold, Hunold, and Gernot slew many warriors in combat before these had really grasped how daring their slayers were, so that afterwards many ladies had to weep for them. Volker, Hagen, and Ortwin, who knew no fear in the fight, dimmed the brightness of numberless helmets with streams of blood in the fray, and Dancwart performed marvels.

And now the men of Denmark tried their hands. You could hear the clang of countless shields under the impact of their charge, and of the sharp swords, too, that were swung there in plenty, while the valiant Saxons also wrought much havoc.

When the Burgundians thrust into the battle they hacked wound on gaping wound, and blood was seen flowing over saddles – so boldly did those knights woo honour. And when the stalwarts from the Netherlands pressed after their lord into the closed ranks of the enemy, their keen swords rang loud and clear as they wielded them – they went in with Siegfried like the splendid young fighting-men they were. Not one of the Rhinelanders was seen to keep up with Siegfried; but as his blows fell you could pick out the rivers of blood running down from his enemy's helmets, till at last he came upon Liudeger at the head of his companions.

Siegfried had cut his way through the enemy there and back for the third time, and now Hagen had come to help him to have his fill of fighting, so that many excellent knights had to die that day from the pair of them. Finding Siegfried before him and seeing him swing his good sword Balmung so high and slay so many of his men, mighty lord Liudeger was seized with fierce anger. There was a grand mêlée and a loud ringing of swords as their retinues closed with each other. Then the two warriors made harsher trial of their prowess, till the Saxons began to give ground. Bitter was the strife between them! The lord of the Saxons had been informed, to his great wrath, that his brother had been taken prisoner, but he was unaware that Siegfried was his captor, since the deed was ascribed to Gernot, though later he learned the truth of it. Liudeger dealt such powerful blows that Siegfried's horse stumbled under him; but when the beast had recovered itself Siegfried raged terribly in the fight, in which he was aided by Hagen, Gernot, Dancwart, and Volker, so that many men lay slain there. Sindold, Hunold, and Sir Ortwin, too, laid low many foemen. These princes were locked in battle. You could see javelins beyond number hurled by warriors' hands flying over helmets and piercing bright shields, with buckler after buckler all stained with blood. Many knights dismounted in the thick of it – Siegfried and Liudeger assailed each other on foot amid flying spears and keen-edged javelins.

Siegfried of the Netherlands was bent on wresting victory from the brave Saxons, of whom many were now wounded, and the weight of his blows sent the bolts and braces flying from their shields. And oh, the bright mail-corselets that Dancwart burst asunder!

Then, suddenly, lord Liudeger descried a crown painted on Siegfried's shield over the grip, and he knew at once that the mighty man was there.

'Stop fighting, all my men!' the warrior shouted to his friends. 'I have just recognized mighty Siegfried, son of Siegmund. The Devil accurst has sent him here to Saxony!' He ordered them to lower their standards, and sued for peace. Peace was later granted him, though, overwhelmed as he had been by fearless Siegfried, he had to be a prisoner in Gunther's land.

[. . .]

Lord Gernot sent messengers to Worms to inform his friends at home of his and his men's success, and how honourably those bold men had acquitted themselves.

The pages spurred hard and made report, and those who had been downcast were overjoyed at the glad news that had reached them, while noble ladies were heard eagerly inquiring how the King's vassals had fared. One of the messengers was summoned into Kriemhild's presence, and this was done in great secrecy – she dared not do it openly, since among those who had fought was the darling of her heart.

When she saw the messenger entering her chamber, lovely Kriemhild said very kindly: 'Tell me the good news, and I will reward you with gold; and if you tell me truly I shall always be your friend. How did my brother Gernot and other of my relations come off in the fighting? Have we perhaps lost many dead? Or, tell me, who acquitted himself best there?'

'There were no cowards on our side anywhere,' the page was quick to answer. 'But, my noble princess, since you have asked me, no man rode so well in battle as our noble guest, brave Siegfried of the Netherlands, who worked miracles there!

[. . .]

No news could have been more welcome to Kriemhild.

'Believe me, my lady,' the page continued, 'more than five hundred able-bodied men are being brought to Burgundy and eighty bloodstained litters of men who are sorely wounded, most of them hewn by brave Siegfried. Those who in their pride sent their challenge to the Rhineland are now perforce Gunther's prisoners, and are being led here with rejoicing.'

A blush suffused Kriemhild's fair cheek when she learned the news, her lovely face blushed red as a rose on hearing that handsome young Siegfried had happily emerged from great peril. She was also glad for her relatives, as indeed she should have been.

'You have brought me good news, and for your pains you shall have some fine clothes and ten marks of gold I shall have fetched for you.' (Such gifts encourage one to tell such news to great ladies.)

[. . .]

By royal command, knightly sports were held continuously, and many young knights followed them with zest. Meanwhile on the riverbank below Worms the King had seats set up for those who had been invited to Burgundy.

Towards the time when the guests were expected, it came to the ears of lovely Kriemhild that her brother wished to give a feast in honour of his esteemed allies, and, accordingly, fair ladies gave assiduous attention to the dresses and wimples they would wear. When queenly Uote heard of the proud knights who had been invited, she had some magnificent fabrics taken from the chest and clothes got ready for love of her dear children; and with these many ladies, maidens, and young warriors of Burgundy were adorned; but she had many fine robes made up for the strangers, too.

5

How Siegfried first set eyes on Kriemhild

Those who wished to attend the festivity could be seen riding towards the Rhine daily, and many who came to Burgundy for love of the King were given chargers and splendid robes. Their high seats were ready for them all at that festival, the noblest and most exalted, to the number, so we are told, of two-and-thirty princes, in expectation of whom fair ladies vied in adorning themselves. Nor was young Giselher idle. He, Gernot, and their suite extended a kindly welcome to friend and stranger alike, saluting the knights with all due ceremony.

Their guests brought with them to this festivity by the Rhine numerous saddles red with gold, and sumptuous shields and robes. Many who had been wounded now appeared cheerful again; while those who were bedridden and harassed by their wounds had to forget death's harshness. But to the loss of those who were languishing the others perforce resigned themselves: one and all, they looked forward with pleasure to the festive days ahead, and to the gay life they meant to lead with the entertainment offered them. Their delight knew no bounds, their hearts overflowed flowed with happiness; and throughout the length and breadth of Gunther's realm there was great rejoicing.

At Whitsuntide one morning, five thousand knights or more emerged from their quarters for the festival to greet the eye with their delightful clothes; and at once in many places the entertainment began, each man striving to outdo his fellow.

The King was observant enough to have noticed how deeply Siegfried loved his sister, though Siegfried had never set eyes on her, whose great beauty was admitted to surpass that of all other young ladies.

Then Ortwin addressed the King. 'If you wish to win full credit at your festivity, you must bring out our lovely maidens for the guests to see – the pride of Burgundy! Where else could a man find delight, if not in pretty girls and fine-looking women? Have your sister appear before the company.' This advice was to the liking of many young warriors.

'I shall be pleased to do so,' replied the King, and all who heard it were deeply gratified. Thus Gunther sent to lady Uote and her beautiful daughter to summon them to court with their young ladies-in-waiting, whereupon bevies of handsome girls chose fine gowns from the coffers and attired themselves with care from stores of noble garments, of bracelets and galloons, which they found in Uote's chest.

Many youthful warriors cherished hopes this day that their looks might please the ladies – good fortune they would not have exchanged for a kingdom! They loved to gaze at women whom they had never seen before.

The noble King commanded a full hundred of his vassals, kinsmen of his and his sister's and members of the Burgundian household, to wait upon her and escort her, sword in hand. And now queenly Uote appeared with Kriemhild, having chosen for company a hundred fair ladies or more, magnificently gowned, while her daughter, too, was attended by a troop of comely maidens.

When these all came into view from their apartment, the knights surged forward with much jostling, in the hope of eyeing the maidens to their hearts' content, if that were possible.

But now lovely Kriemhild emerged like the dawn from the dark clouds, freeing from much distress him who secretly cherished her and indeed long had done so. He saw the adorable maiden stand there in all her splendour – gems past counting gleamed from her robe, while her rosy cheeks glowed bewitchingly; so that even if a man were to have his heart's desire he could not claim to have seen anything fairer. Kriemhild outshone many good ladies as the moon the stars when its light shines clear from the sky, and those gallant warriors' hearts rose within them as they gazed on her.

Stately chamberlains preceded her, but the spirited knights would not desist from pressing forward to where they could glimpse the charming girl. As to Siegfried, he was both glad and sad. 'How could it ever happen that I should win your love?' he asked himself. 'This is a foolish self-deception. But I would rather I were dead than shun your company.' At these thoughts his colour came and went.

Siegfried son of Siegmund stood there handsome as though limned on parchment with all a master's skill (as indeed it was admitted that none was his equal for looks).

Those who were escorting the ladies bade the knights

make way everywhere, and many of them complied. And as they observed all these fine women with their well-bred ways, the high aspirations in their hearts brought joy to many men.

Then lord Gernot of Burgundy spoke. 'Gunther, dear brother, you must make a like return in the presence of all these warriors to the man who gave his services so kindly, nor shall I ever blush for having counselled it. Present Siegfried to my sister, so that the maiden may accord him her greeting – we shall never cease to reap the benefit. Although she has never addressed a knight before, let her now bid Siegfried welcome. With this we shall attach this splendid warrior to ourselves.'

Kinsmen of Gunther went over to where the hero of the Netherlands was standing, and said: 'The King gives you leave to enter his presence, for he wishes to honour you with his sister's salutation.'

Lord Siegfried was delighted in his heart, which now nourished joy without sorrow, for he was to meet fair Uote's daughter. And indeed she greeted him becomingly.

When the proud man stood before her, she saw his face take fire. 'You are welcome lord Siegfried, noble knight,' said she. Siegfried's spirits soared at this greeting, and he bowed his devoted thanks. Then she took him by the hand, and how ardently did this lord walk beside the lady, exchanging tender looks with her in secret!

If a white hand were pressed there affectionately at the promptings of sweet love, then I was not told so; yet I cannot believe that it was not, for she had soon conveyed her liking; so that in days of summer or at the approach of May, Siegfried had never had cause for such ecstasy as now, as he walked hand in hand with her whom he wished to wed.

'Ah, if only this had happened to me,' thought many a knight, 'that I should walk at her side as I have seen him do – or even lie beside her! I should not quarrel with that.' Yet no warrior served better to win a queen than Siegfried.

Whichever lands they were from, the guests had eyes for those two alone. Leave was granted for her to bestow a kiss on the handsome man, and never in all his life had anything so pleasant befallen him.

'This most exalted kiss has been the cause of many a man's lying wounded from Siegfried's strong arm, as I know to my cost,' the King of Denmark interposed quickly. 'May God never permit him to enter my kingdom.'

The courtiers everywhere were ordered to fall back and make way for fair Kriemhild, and then a company of brave knights took her decorously to church. But, arriving there, handsome Siegfried was parted from her, while she entered the minster with her train of ladies, making such a picture in all her finery that many knights picked her out to feast their eyes, nursing hopes as vain as they were lofty.

Siegfried could scarce wait till mass had been sung. He had reason to bless his good fortune that the young woman whom he cherished in his thoughts was so well-disposed towards him; and indeed there was no small reason why he should love the beautiful girl. When she came out of church, Siegfried was there in advance of her, and they asked the brave knight to rejoin her.

Only now did charming Kriemhild thank him for having fought so magnificently at the head of her kinsmen. 'May God reward you, lord Siegfried', said the lovely girl, 'for having earned from our knights such loyal devotion as I hear them speak of.'

'I shall always be at their service,' he answered, with a loving look at Kriemhild, 'and, unless death prevents me, I will never rest my head before I have done their pleasure. This I do to win your favour, my lady Kriemhild.'

Each day for the space of twelve, the excellent young woman was seen in Siegfried's company when she had to appear at court in the presence of her relatives, a compliment they paid him in the hope that it would give him much pleasure. And daily there was great merriment below Gunther's hall and the happy clamour, both outside and within, of a crowd of bold men jousting. Ortwin and Hagen performed great feats; for whatever pursuit anyone wished to follow these gay knights were ready for it with all their heart, so that they became well known to the guests, and the whole land reaped glory from it.

Those who had been wounded came outside and sought entertainment with the company at fencing under the shield and at javelin-throwing, and numerous strong men joined in with them.

The King regaled them all with the choicest viands at this feast; he had placed himself beyond all such reproach as kings may incur. Going up to his guests, he addressed them in friendly fashion. 'Before you leave you must accept my gifts, good knights,' he said, 'for it is my thought that if you do not disdain them I shall be forever obliged. I shall be heartily glad to share my wealth with you.'

'Before we ride home to our country,' answered the Danes immediately, 'we wish to make peace with you firmly; and not without good reason, since we have lost many dear friends whom your knights have slain.' Though Liudegast was now healed of his wounds and the lord of the Saxons too had recovered from the hurts of battle, they were leaving some few dead in Burgundy.

King Gunther went to Siegfried. 'Advise me what to do,' he said. 'Our opponents wish to ride home to-morrow morning, and are asking me and my vassals for a firm treaty of peace. Now you must advise me, brave Siegfried, which course you think the best. Let me tell you what these lords are offering me. If I were to set them free, they would be pleased to give me as much gold as can be carried by five hundred sumpters.'

'That would be wrong,' said mighty Siegfried. 'You must allow the noble warriors to go free of obligations on the understanding that in future they must refrain from invading your country. Let both give you this assurance on their royal oaths.'

'I shall follow this advice.' Thereupon they left that place. And it was announced to Gunther's enemies that nobody wanted the gold which they had offered. (How their dear relations at home longed to see these battleworn men!)

Shield after shield full of gold was carried in, and, on Gernot's advice, Gunther doled it out copiously to his friends in unweighed heaps of about five hundred marks, and to some of them even more. Then, when they were on the point of departing, all the guests took leave of the King and they also appeared before Kriemhild, and before Queen Uote's throne; and never were knights dismissed with greater honour.

When they rode away, the guests' quarters were empty; but the King remained at home in his magnificence together with his many noble kinsmen, who daily came to wait on lady Kriemhild.

Then, in despair of achieving his purpose, Siegfried wished to take his leave, and it came to the King's ears that he was intending to depart. But youthful Giselher dissuaded him from going.

'Where did you intend to ride off to, most noble Siegfried? Do as I ask you and stay with us knights, with King Gunther and his vassals. There are many beautiful ladies here with whose acquaintance we shall be pleased to honour you.'

'Then do not fetch the horses,' mighty Siegfried commanded. 'I was meaning to ride away, but I shall not do so – and take our shields away! – I was planning to return to my country. But lord Giselher has turned me from my purpose in the loyal affection that he bears me.'

And so, to please his friends, the valiant man remained: nor was there another land anywhere in which he might have sojourned so agreeably; with the result that, now, he saw Kriemhild every day. It was her transcendent beauty that caused lord Siegfried to stay there.

They passed the time with all manner of amusements, except that, time and time again, he was tormented by the passion she aroused in him, thanks to which, in days to come, the hero met a pitiful end.

6

How Gunther sailed to Iceland for Brunhild

Tidings never heard before had crossed the Rhine, telling how, beyond it, there lived many lovely maidens. Good King Gunther conceived the idea of winning one, and his heart thrilled at the thought of it.

Over the sea there dwelt a queen whose like was never known, for she was of vast strength and surpassing beauty. With her love as the prize, she vied with brave warriors at throwing the javelin, and the noble lady also hurled the weight to a great distance and followed with a long leap; and whoever aspired to her love had, without fail, to win these three tests against her, or else, if he lost but one, he forfeited his head.

The maiden had competed in this way times out of number; and having heard this report in his kingdom on the Rhine, the handsome knight turned his thoughts to winning the lovely woman, for which brave warriors had to die in the end.

'Whatever fate is in store for me,' said the lord of the Rhenish land, 'I shall sail down to the sea and go to Brunhild. To win her love I mean to stake my life and indeed I shall lose it if I fail to make her mine.'

'I would advise against that,' said Siegfried. 'This queen has such terrible ways that it costs any man dear who woos her, so that truly you should forgo this journey.'

'In that case,' interposed Hagen, 'I should advice you to ask Siegfried to share these perils with you, seeing that he is so knowledgeable about Brunhild's affairs.'

'Will you help me woo this handsome woman, noble Siegfried?' asked Gunther. 'If you do as I ask, and I win her for my love, I will stake my life and honour for you in turn.'

'I will do it, if you will give me your sister fair Kriemhild, the noble princess,' answered Siegfried, Siegmund's son. 'I wish no other reward for my trouble.'

'I agree to that,' replied Gunther. 'Siegfried, here is my hand on it! If fair Brunhild comes to this country I will give you my sister to wife, and you can live in joy with the lovely girl always.'

The exalted knights swore oaths on it; and this added mightily to their toils, for great were the dangers they had to face before they brought the lady to Burgundy.

They now made preparations for their voyage. Siegfried would have to take with him the magic cloak which he had won so manfully from the dwarf Alberich, and at such peril. Wearing it, he gained the strength of twelve beyond that of his own powerful frame. He wooed the splendid woman with great subtlety, since the cloak was of such a kind that without being seen any man could do as he pleased in it. In this way he won Brunhild, though he had cause to rue it later.

'Now tell me, Siegfried, brave knight, before I start on my journey, must we take a retinue to Brunhild's land in order to go to sea with full honours? Thirty thousand knights can soon be mustered.'

'However great an army we take, the Queen has such dreadful ways that they would all have to die through her arrogance. Let me propose something better, good warrior. Let us sail down the Rhine like soldiers of fortune, and let me name those who are to form the party. We shall put to sea four in all and so win the lady, whatever becomes of us afterwards. Now, I shall be one of these companions, and you be the second; let Hagen be the third, and brave Dancwart the fourth. In this way we shall escape with our lives, for a thousand others would not face us in battle!'

'Before we leave,' said King Gunther, 'I should very much like to know what sort of clothes we must wear at Brunhild's court – tell me that.'

'In Brunhild's land they always wear the very best clothes you ever saw, and so we must appear splendidly dressed at her court lest we be disgraced when the news of our arrival is brought.'

'Then I shall go to my dear mother,' answered the good knight, 'and see if I can obtain leave for those pretty girls of hers to help us to get ready such clothes as we can wear with distinction when we appear before noble Brunhild.'

'Why do you ask your mother for such services?' asked Hagen of Troneck in his lordly way. 'Tell your sister what you have in mind – her help will turn out well for you on this visit to Brunhild's court.'

Gunther accordingly sent a message to his sister to say that he and Siegfried wished to see her. But before this was done the lovely girl dressed herself exquisitely – it was only with mild regret that she viewed the warriors' coming! And now her train, too, were adorned becomingly. The two princes then entered; hearing which, Kriemhild rose from her seat and politely went to receive her noble visitor and her brother.

'You are welcome, brother, and your companion, too!' said the maiden. 'I should like to know what prompts you lords to seek my presence? Tell me, what brings you noble warriors here?'

'I will indeed, my lady,' answered King Gunther. 'Despite our gay aspirations we have grounds for anxiety too, since we intend to go travelling to distant lands in order to pay court to the ladies, and we need elegant clothes for our journey.'

'Be seated, dear brother,' said the princess, 'and tell me all about those ladies whose love you desire in other lands.' And she took the illustrious pair by the hand and led them to the sumptuous couch on which she had been sitting and whose covers, you may believe me, were embroidered in gold with fine pictures.

It was pleasant passing the time here with the ladies. As to Siegfried and Kriemhild, they had ample opportunity for kind looks and friendly glances. He cherished her in his heart, for she was as dear to him as life; and indeed in the end fair Kriemhild became strong Siegfried's wife.

'Dearest sister,' said the great King, 'we mean to pass the time in dalliance in Brunhild's country, and we need some fine clothes to wear before the ladies. But unless you help us this will not be possible.'

'I shall leave you in no doubt, dear brother, that I

am ready to do anything within my power for you,' answered the young lady, 'and I should be very sorry if any other were to deny you. You must not ask so timidly but command me as my lord, since I am at your service for whatever you care to ask of me. I shall do it gladly,' the charming girl concluded.

'We wish to wear good clothes, sister, and you must help us to prepare them with your own noble hands. Let your girls complete the task, so that our clothes suit us well – for go on this journey we must!'

'Listen to me,' said the young lady. 'Silk I have myself; but you get your men to fetch us jewels by the shieldful, and then we shall stitch your clothes.' To this Gunther and Siegfried assented. 'But who are the companions that are to go to court with you in grand array?' continued the Princess.

'There are four of us all told,' he answered. 'Two of my men, Hagen and Dancwart, must accompany me to court. Now mark what I am telling you, my lady; we four are to wear three different sets of clothes a day for four days, and of such quality that we can quit Brunhild's land without disgrace.'

Their lordships withdrew after taking kind leave of Princess Kriemhild, who then summoned from her apartments thirty of her maidens that were gifted for such work. They threaded precious stones into snow-white silk from Arabia or into silk from Zazamanc as green as clover, making fine robes, while noble Kriemhild cut the cloth herself. Whatever handsome linings they could lay hands on from the skins of strange water-beasts, wondrous to see, they covered with silk, just as the knights would wear them. And now hear some marvellous things about their dazzling clothes.

The ladies were well supplied with the best Moroccan and Libyan silk that a royal family ever acquired, and Kriemhild let it be seen clearly that these knights enjoyed her favour. And now that they had set their hearts on this voyage with its lofty goal, furs of ermine no longer seemed good enough: their linings were covered instead with coal-black brocades all spangled with brilliant stones set in Arabian gold such as would well become brave warriors on festive occasions today. The noble ladies had not been idle, since in the space of seven weeks they had finished the garments, by which time the good knights' armour, too, was ready. And now that their preparations were over, a stout bark that had been carefully built for them stood ready on the Rhine to carry them downstream to the open sea. The noble young ladies were spent with their toil; but they sent word to the knights to say that their work was done, and that the elegant clothes which they had wished to take with them were ready to their requirements.

Then the King and his men wished to tarry by the Rhine no longer, and he sent a messenger to the companions to ask them if they would like to see their new clothes and try them on. The clothes fitted them perfectly, and the warriors thanked the ladies. And all to whom they showed themselves had to admit never having seen anything better, so that they could wear them at court with pleasure. Theirs was the best of knightly apparel, and they thanked Kriemhild profusely.

Then these high-hearted warriors asked leave to depart with all knightly decorum, making bright eyes moist and dim with tears.

'Dearest brother,' Kriemhild said, 'if you would stay here, where your life would not be in such danger, and woo other ladies, I should say it was well done. You can find her equal nearer home.'

I imagine the ladies' hearts foretold them the outcome, since whatever anyone said to them they wept, one and all, so that the gold above their breasts was dulled by the copious tears they shed.

'Lord Siegfried,' said Kriemhild, 'let me commend my dear brother to your loyal protection so that no harm befalls him in Brunhild's land.'

The dauntless man gave Lady Kriemhild his hand and swore it. 'If I remain alive, madam,' he said, 'you shall be rid of all your cares. I shall bring him back here to the Rhine unscathed, rely on it!' The lovely maiden inclined her head in thanks.

Their shields that shone with gold were carried on to the riverbank, and all their gear was brought. And now word was given for their chargers to be led out, for they were ready to go. At this fair ladies wept abundantly, while charming young girls thronged the windows.

A strong wind in the sail sent a shudder through the ship, and the proud companions embarked on the Rhine.

'Who will be captain?' said King Gunther.

'I,' answered Siegfried. 'I can pilot you over the deep, believe me, good warriors, for the right sea paths are well known to me.' Thus they were leaving Burgundy in good heart. Siegfried quickly seized a sweep and pushed off powerfully from the bank. King Gunther himself took an oar, and so these excellent knights put her out from land.

They had on board with them choice food and excellent wine, indeed the best Rhenish to be had; their horses were well stabled and they themselves were very comfortable; their craft sailed on an even keel, and they met nothing untoward; their stout halyards were hauled taut: and so before a good wind they sailed twenty miles down-stream by nightfall (though later these proud warriors were to rue their toil).

By the twelfth morning, so we are told, the winds had carried them far away to Isenstein in Brunhild's land, which none but Siegfried knew. Seeing so many walled cities and the broad domains, King Gunther swiftly said: 'Tell me, friend Siegfried, do you know whose cities and fien lands these are?'

'Indeed I do,' answered Siegfried. 'They are Brunhild's land and people and the fortress of Isenstein, of which I told you; and before this day is out you shall see many lovely women there. But I would counsel you; knights, for it seems advisable to me, to be of one mind and all say the same thing, since when later today we enter Queen Brunhild's presence we must inevitably go in great fear of her. When we see the adorable woman with her retainers about her, noble warriors, you must abide by this one story – that Gunther is my overlord and I am his vassal. Then all his hopes will come true.'

They agreed to all that Siegfried bade them promise, and none refrained out of pride from saying whatever he wanted, so that things went well with them when King Gunther met fair Brunhild.

'I undertake to do this not so much from affection for you as for the sake of your beautiful sister,' said Siegfried. 'I love her as my own life and soul, and I shall serve gladly to this end, that she shall marry me.'

7

How Gunther won Brunhild

Their bark had now sailed near enough to the fortress for King Gunther to see troops of lovely maidens standing at the windows above, and he was sorry that none of them was known to him.

'Do you know anything about those girls looking down at us here on the water?' he asked his comrade Siegfried. 'Whatever the name of their lord, they look spirited young women.'

'Take secret stock of the young ladies,' replied lord Siegfried, 'and tell me which you would take, if you could choose.'

'I shall,' answered the bold knight. 'Now I can see one standing at the window there in a snow-white gown who is so beautiful that my eyes have singled her out, so that had I the power to choose I should assuredly make her my wife.'

'Your eyes have chosen very fittingly, for that lovely girl is noble Brunhild, to whom your whole being is so ardently drawn.' And indeed, Gunther liked everything about her.

Then the Queen told her superb young ladies to move away from the windows – they were not to stand there as a spectacle for strangers. They obediently did as they were told. But we have since learnt what these ladies did. They put on their finery to receive these unknown visitors, as comely women have always done, and, prompted by their curiosity, went up to the loopholes and through them took note of the warriors. Only four had entered their country.

Through their peep-holes those handsome women saw bold Siegfried lead a war-horse ashore, which to Gunther's way of thinking much enhanced his own importance. The horse was big and strong as it was handsome, and Siegfried held the magnificent beast by its bridle till King Gunther was seated in the saddle, such service did Siegfried render him; though the time was to come when Gunther had utterly forgotten it. Then Siegfried fetched his own horse from the ship; but never had he done such duty before as to hold a warrior's stirrup for him. All of this was seen by those proud and comely women through the loopholes.

The horses and robes of this gay pair of knights were of the very same dazzling snow-white hue; their fine shields shone in their grasp; their gem-studded saddles and narrow poitrels were hung with bells of lustrous red gold: thus magnificently did they come riding up to Brunhild's hall. These handsome knights arrived in her country, as their high courage demanded, with newly ground spear-heads and splendid swords that reached down to their spurs and were both broad and sharp. Such weapons did they wear, and none of this was lost on noble Brunhild.

With them came Dancwart and Hagen, and we are told that these warriors wore rich clothes as black as the raven, with fine great shields. You could see the Indian jewels they were wearing on their robes move in gorgeous ripples as they walked.

The good warriors had left their bark beside the sea unguarded, and were riding up to the castle, within whose walls they saw eighty-six towers, three great palaces and a splendid hall of noble, grass-green marble, where Brunhild waited with her court.

The fortress was opened and the gates were flung wide, and Brunhild's vassals ran out to meet them and to welcome them to their lady's country. Word was given to take their horses and shields to be cared for. 'You must give us your swords and bright corselets,' said one of the chamberlains.

'You shall not have them,' answered Hagen of Troneck. 'We will carry them ourselves.'

But Siegfried intervened to enlighten him. 'In this castle, let me tell you, it is the custom that no guest shall wear his armour. Now let them take yours away, that would be the right thing to do.' Gunther's man Hagen complied, yet much against his will.

They ordered drink to be poured for the guests and gave them comfortable quarters. Many brave warriors in princely clothes were to be seen at court there, coming and going in all directions; yet the appearance of the bold strangers attracted great attention.

It was then reported to lady Brunhild that unknown knights clad in magnificent robes had arrived after a sea-voyage, and the good maiden began to ask questions. 'Tell me who these strange knights may be,' said the fair Queen, 'that stand within my walls in such stately array, and for whose sake they have made the journey here.'

'I dare assert, my lady,' said one of her court, 'that I have never set eyes on any of them, save that one of them bears a likeness to Siegfried. I earnestly advise you to receive him kindly. The second of the companions has this distinction, that he could be a mighty king holding sway over great principalities, if they were his for the ruling; for he stands so majestically beside the others. The third, though of handsome appearance, mighty Queen, strikes terror with his vehement glances which he darts ceaselessly about him, so that I fancy his is a fierce humour. Of the youngest this can be said to his praise, that I saw the noble knight standing there as modest as a maid, excellent in his bearing and altogether charming; yet we should have cause to be afraid if anyone here provoked him, for however engaging his manners, and however handsome his looks, he has it in him to bereave many fair women, once his blood is up. He has the whole appearance of a fearless knight in all that goes to make one.'

'Bring me my robes,' said the Queen. 'If strong Siegfried has come it is at peril of his life, since I do not fear him so much that I should consent to marry him.'

Fair Brunhild was soon beautifully attired, and then, accompanied by bevies of pretty girls, a full hundred or more and all of them elegantly dressed, she went. For these comely ladies were curious to see the strangers. Brunhild's warriors, knights of Iceland to the number of five hundred or more, attended them sword in hand, a sight far from pleasing to the visitors, who nevertheless rose from their seats undismayed and undaunted. Now pray listen to what this maiden-queen said when she saw Siegfried. 'Welcome, Siegfried, to my country. I should very much like to know what brings you here.'

'You accord me too much favour, my lady Brunhild, magnanimous Queen, when you deign to salute me before this noble knight, who, as befits my lord, stands nearer to you than I – an honour I would gladly forgo! My liege is a prince of the Rhenish lands – what more need I tell you? – and we have voyaged here to win your love. For whatever the fate in store for him he means to make you his wife. Now consider this while there is time, since my lord means to hold you to your terms. His name is Gunther, and he is a king most high. If he were to win your love, he would have nothing left to wish for. The handsome warrior commanded me to sail here, but, had it been in my power to deny him, I would gladly have refrained.'

'If he is your lord and you are his liegeman, and provided he dares essay my sports (whose rules I shall lay down for him) and proves himself the winner, I shall wed him. Otherwise, if I win, it will cost you all your lives!'

'Madam, show us your formidable contests,' said Hagen of Troneck. 'It would have to go hard with my lord Gunther before he would own you had beaten him. He trusts himself to win a handsome young woman such as you.'

'He will have to cast the weight, follow through with a leap, and then throw the javelin with me. Do not be too hasty – you may well lose your lives and reputations here,' said the charming woman. 'Consider it very closely.'

Brave Siegfried went up to the King and told him not to be afraid, but to speak his whole mind to the Queen. 'With the aid of my ruses I shall see that she does you no harm.'

'Most noble Queen,' replied King Gunther, 'lay down whatever rules you like. Even were there more to come, I would face them all for love of your fair person. If I fail to make you my wife, then let me lose my head!'

Having heard Gunther's words, the Queen commanded them make haste with the games, this being her good pleasure. She sent for a stout suit of armour, a corselet of ruddy gold, and a good shield. She drew on a silken gambeson beautifully fashioned from Libyan brocade that no weapon ever pierced in battle, agleam with dazzling orfrays.

All this time the Burgundian knights were being threatened and taunted, so that Dancwart and Hagen were far from pleased and were troubled in their hearts how the King might fare. 'This journey of ours does not look too good for us,' they thought.

Meanwhile, before any could notice it, handsome Siegfried had returned to their ship to fetch his magic cloak from its hiding-place, and, quickly slipping into it, he was invisible to all. Hurrying back, he found many warriors assembled where the Queen was explaining her hazardous sports, and thanks to his magic wiles he rejoined them secretly and unseen.

The ring was marked out in which the games were to be witnessed by over seven hundred bold fighting-men that were seen there under arms and would declare who had won the contest.

And now Brunhild had arrived, armed as though about to contend for all the kingdoms in the world and wearing many tiny bars of gold over her silk, against which her lovely face shone radiantly. Next came her retainers, bearing a great, broad shield of reddest gold, with braces of hardest steel, under which the enchanting maiden meant to dispute the issue. For its baldrick her shield had a fine silk cord studded with grass-green gems whose variegated lustre vied with the gold of their settings. The man whom she would favour would have to be a very brave one: for this shield which the girl was to carry was (so we are told) a good three spans thick beneath the boss; it was resplendent with steel and with gold, and even with the help of three others her chamberlain could scarce raise it.

'What now, King Gunther?' stalwart Hagen of Troneck asked fiercely, on seeing the shield brought out. 'We are done for – the woman whose love you desire is a rib of the Devil himself!'

You must hear more about her attire, with which she was amply provided. The Queen wore a magnificent tabard of silk of Azagouc, from which shone many precious stones, adding their lustre to hers.

They thereupon carried out for the lady a great spear, both sharp and heavy, which she was accustomed to throw – it was strong, and of huge proportions, and dreadfully keen at its edges. And now listen to this extraordinary thing about the weight of that spear: a good three-and-a-half ingots had gone into its forging, and three of Brunhild's men could scarcely lift it, so that noble Gunther was deeply alarmed. 'What will come of this?' he wondered. 'How could the Devil from Hell survive it? If I were safe and sound again in Burgundy, she would not be bothered by my wooing till Doomsday!'

'I heartily regret our visit to this court,' said bold Dancwart, Hagen's brother. 'We have always borne the name of heroes, but what a shameful way of dying if we are to perish at the hands of women! I bitterly rue ever having come to this country. But if my brother Hagen and I had our swords in our hands, all these vassals of Brunhild would have to tread gently with their arrogance. And know this for sure: they would do well to repress it, for had I sworn a thousand oaths to keep the peace, that bewitching young lady would have to lose her life before I would see my dear lord die!'

'If we had our battle gear and our trusty swords,' replied his brother Hagen, 'we should certainly leave this country as free men, and this amazon's proud spirit would be mollified.'

The noble maiden heard the warrior's words, and, looking over her shoulder, she said with a smile: 'Since he fancies himself to be so brave, bring these knights their armour, and give them their sharp swords too.'

When they had regained possession of their swords, as the maiden had commanded, bold Dancwart flushed with joy. 'Let them do what sports they like,' he said. 'Now that we have our swords, Gunther will remain unbeaten!'

Brunhild's strength was clearly tremendous, for they brought a heavy boulder to the ring for her, round, and of monstrous size – twelve lusty warriors could barely carry it! – and this she would always hurl after throwing her javelin. The Burgundians' fears rose high at the sight of it. 'Mercy on us!' said Hagen. 'What sort of a lover has the King got here? Rather should she be the Devil's drab in Hell!'

She furled her sleeves over her dazzling white arms, took a grip on her shield, snatched her spear aloft, and the contest was on! Gunther and Siegfried went in fear of her enmity, and she would have taken the King's life, had not Siegfried come to his aid. But Siegfried went up to him unseen and touched his hand, startling him with his magic powers. 'What was it that touched me?' the brave man wondered, looking all around him, yet finding no one there. 'It is I, your dear friend Siegfried,' said the other. 'You must not fear the Queen. Give me your shield, and let me bear it, and take careful note of what I say to you. Now, you go through the motions, and I shall do the deeds.' Gunther was relieved when he recognized him. 'Keep my wiles a secret,' continued Siegfried, 'and tell nobody about them, then the Queen will get little of the glory which she nevertheless hopes to win from you. Just see how coolly she faces you!'

Thereupon the noble maiden let fly with great power at the large, new shield which the son of Sieglind bore, so that sparks leapt up from the steel as though fanned by the wind, while the blade of the stout javelin tore clean through the shield, and a tongue of fire flared up from Gunther's mailshirt. Those strong men reeled under the shock, and, but for the magic cloak, they would have died there and then. Blood spurted from

Siegfried's mouth, but he quickly rebounded, and, taking the spear which she had cast through his shield, the powerful warrior sent it back at her. 'I do not wish to would or kill the lovely girl,' he thought, and reversing the spear so that its point was now behind him, he hurled the shaft with such manly vigour that it went straight through to her corselet with a mighty clang, and sent the sparks flying from the chain-mail as though driven by the wind. Siegmund's son put such lusty strength into his throw that, for all her might, she failed to keep her feet under its impact – an exploit, I swear, which King Gunther would never have accomplished.

But Brunhild swiftly leapt up again. 'My compliments on that throw, Gunther, noble knight!' said she, imagining that had Gunther achieved it with his own strength; but the man who was on her tracks was far mightier than he.

The noble maiden hastened up to the mark, for she was very angry now, and, raising the stone on high, flung it with great force a long stretch away from her, then followed her throw with a leap that set all her harness ringing. The boulder had fallen a good twenty-four yards away – but the fair maiden's leap exceeded it! Lord Siegfried went to where the great stone lay. Gunther took the strain of it, but it was brave Siegfried who did the throwing.

Siegfried was a valiant man. He was tall, and of powerful build. He hurled the boulder farther, and he surpassed it with his leap; and, thanks to his wonderful magic powers, he had the strength as he sprang to take King Gunther with him.

The leap was done, the stone had come to rest. None was to be seen other than doughty King Gunther, from whom Siegfried had warded off death. Fair Brunhild flushed red with anger. Seeing the warrior unscathed at his side of the ring, she said to her retainers in a voice not altogether quiet: 'Come forward at once, my kinsmen and vassals! You must do homage to King Gunther.' Then those brave men laid down their weapons and knelt before the great King Gunther of Burgundy in large numbers, in the belief that it was he who with his unaided strength had performed those feats.

Gunther saluted the illustrious maiden pleasantly, for he was a man of fine breeding. Then, clasping him by the hand, Brunhild gave him express authority to rule over her country, much to warlike Hagen's pleasure.

And now Brunhild desired the noble knight to go with her to her spacious palace, and when they arrived there the Burgundian warriors were shown all the greater courtesy, so that Dancwart and Hagen had to put their anger by. As to brave Siegfried, he had the prudence to take his magic cloak and stow it away again, after which he returned to where the ladies were assembled.

'What are you waiting for, Sire?' the resourceful man asked the King, pretending he did not know, and thereby showing his sagacity. 'Why do you not begin the games, of which the Queen is setting so many for you? Let us soon see what they are like.'

'How did it happen, lord Siegfried,' asked the Queen, 'that you did not witness the games that Gunther won here?'

'You made us nervous, madam,' replied Hagen, 'and so while the Rhenish Prince was winning the games from you, Siegfried was down by our ship – that is why he does not know.'

'I am delighted to hear that your pride has been lowered in this way,' said brave Siegfried, 'and that there is someone alive who can master you. You must come to the Rhine with us now, noble maiden.'

'This cannot be done before my kinsmen and vassals are acquainted with it,' replied handsome Brunhild. 'You must know I cannot leave my country so lightly without first summoning those who are nearest me.' She then sent messengers riding in all directions to summon the kinsmen and vassals on whom she most relied, requesting them to come to Isenstein at once. And indeed, day by day, morning and evening, they came riding to Brunhild's fortress by companies.

'Good Heavens!' said Hagen. 'What have we done? This is asking for trouble, waiting here like this for fair Brunhild's men to arrive! Once they are here in force – we do not know the Queen's intentions – what if she be so furious that she is plotting our destruction? – the noble maiden may prove our undoing!'

'I shall prevent it,' said mighty Siegfried. 'I shall not let your fears come true. I shall bring rare warriors here to your aid whom you have never met before. Do not ask after me, for I shall sail away; and may God preserve your honour in the meantime! I shall return with all speed, bringing with me a thousand of the very best fighting-men I know.'

'Well, do not be too long,' replied the King. 'We are very glad of your help, and rightly so.'

'I shall return within a very few days. And tell Brunhild that it was you who dispatched me.'

8

How Siegfried sailed to fetch his vassals

Hidden in his magic cloak, Siegfried left by the gate that opened on to the shore. There he found a bark, and, boarding it unseen, sculled it swiftly away as though the wind were blowing it. None could see the helmsman, yet, propelled by Siegfried's huge strength, the little craft made such headway that people thought a gale must be blowing it. But no, it was being sculled by Siegfried, fair Sieglind's son.

After voyaging for the rest of that day and on into the night for upwards of a hundred miles, Siegfried thanks to his vast exertions reached a land that was named after the Nibelungs, of whose great treasure he was lord. Alone though he was, the dauntless warrior sailed to a large island in the river, quickly moored the bark, and made for a castle on a hill in quest of shelter, as is the way with travel-weary men.

Arriving before the gateway he found it barred, for those within were punctilious in discharge of their duty, as people still are today. The stranger fell to pounding on the gate, but the gate was well guarded – he saw standing inside a gigantic watchman, whose arms always lay near to hand.

'Who is that pounding on the gate so mightily?' asked the warden.

'A soldier of fortune! Come, throw open the portal!' answered lord Siegfried from the other side, disguising his voice. 'Before the day is out I shall rouse the fighting-spirit of some few out here who would prefer to lie snug and at ease!' The gatekeeper was annoyed to hear lord Siegfried say so.

In a trice the giant had donned his armour, put on his helmet, snatched up his shield, and flung open the gate; and how ferociously the burly man rushed at Siegfried! How dare this visitor wake so many warriors! And he began to lay about him with his iron pole, forcing the noble stranger to seek cover under his shield, whose braces this watchman yet managed to shatter. This brought the hero into great peril, so that Siegfried was in no small fear of being killed by the mighty blows of this gatekeeper – a feat that much endeared the man to his liege lord Siegfried!

They fought so fiercely that the whole castle re-echoed and the din was heard in the hall of the Nibelungs. Yet Siegfried overcame the watchman and afterwards bound him, news of which went round all Nibelungland.

Far away through the cavern the fearless kobold Alberich heard this savage fight, and, arming himself at once, rushed to where the noble stranger had laid the giant in bonds. Alberich was very strong and of ferocious temper; he wore a helmet, and chain-mail on his body, and wielded a scourge heavy with gold and on whose thongs seven massive balls were hung. Running at great speed towards Siegfried, he struck such bitter blows at the shield which the hero was gripping that large parts of it were smashed, and Siegfried feared for his life. Flinging his ruined shield aside, the handsome stranger thrust his long sword into its sheath, remembering his good breeding as decency required; for he was loath to slay his own treasurer. Thus, with only his strong hands to help him, he leapt at Alberich, seized the old man by his grey beard, and roughly dragged him to and fro till he shrieked at the top of his voice. This chastisement by the young hero was a painful thing for Alberich.

'Let me live!' cried the dwarf, who was both brave and subtle. 'If I could be the bondman of any man except only that one warrior whose subject I swore to be, I would serve you, rather than die!'

He bound Alberich as he had bound the giant before him, and much did Alberich suffer from his might.

'Who are you?' the dwarf managed to ask.

'I am Siegfried. I thought I was well known to you.'

'I am very glad to hear it!' replied Alberich. 'I have now made the acquaintance of your heroic handiwork and see that you are indeed fit to be a sovereign lord. If you let me live I shall do all that you command.'

'Go quickly, and bring me the best fighting-men we have, to the number of a thousand Nibelungs. They are to come and see me here.' But none heard him declare just why he wanted this done.

He loosed the giant's and Alberich's bonds, and the latter made haste and found the warriors. With fear still upon him, he roused the Nibelungs. 'Get up, you warriors!' he cried. 'You must go to Siegfried.' They jumped up from their beds with alacrity; and when a thousand brave knights had donned their fine clothes, they repaired to where Siegfried was standing, and gave him a warm welcome with formal show of their allegiance. Many candles were lit, and a spiced wine was poured for him. He thanked them for coming so promptly. 'You must sail away over the sea with me,' he told those good warriors, and he found them most willing to do so.

Three thousand knights had hastened there, of whom a thousand of the best were chosen. Their helmets and other harness were brought for them, since it was Siegfried's intention to take them to Brunhild's land.

'You good knights,' he said, 'listen to what I have to tell you. You must wear magnificent robes to court, since we are to appear before many beauties there – so adorn yourselves in fine clothes!'

Early one morning they put to sea. What gallant companions Siegfried had enlisted! – they had good mounts and splendid accoutrements on board with them and they arrived in Brunhild's country with much pomp. And there, standing on the battlements, were the lovely maidens.

'Does anyone know who those men are, whom I see sailing far out at sea?' asked the Queen. 'They carry magnificent sails, whiter even than snow.'

'They are my men,' answered the King of the Rhineland. 'I left them near at hand as I sailed here. I sent for them, and now they have arrived, my lady.'

The noble strangers came in for very close scrutiny. Then Siegfried, splendidly attired, was seen standing forward in the ship in the company of many others.

'My lord King,' said the Queen, 'kindly tell me whether

I am to receive these strangers or withhold my greeting from them.'

'You should go to meet them in front of the palace, so that they may know we are pleased to see them,' he replied. She did as he advised her, according Siegfried a separate greeting. Lodgement was provided for them, and their gear was safely stored. So many foreigners had entered the country that they were thronging the place in crowds, here, there, and everywhere.

But now the brave knights wished to sail home to Burgundy.

'I should be obliged to anyone who could dole out my treasure of both silver and gold among my guests and the King's,' said the Queen.

'Let me take care of the keys, most noble Queen,' answered bold Giselher's vassal Dancwart. 'I vow I shall distribute it in such a way that any disgrace I incur will be entirely due to me.' The brave knight made it very plain that he was generously inclined.

When Hagen's brother had taken charge of the keys he lavished magnificent gifts; and if any asked for a mark he gave them so much that all who were poor and needy could live happily on it. Over and over again he bestowed a hundred pounds or more at a time; and many who had never worn such fine clothes in their lives walked past that hall arrayed in splendid robes. But when the Queen came to hear of it, believe me, she was piqued.

'My lord King,' said that proud lady, 'I could do without your treasurer's generosity, since he intends not to leave me a stitch and is frittering away all my gold. I should be eternally obliged to any who would put a stop to it. This knight is lavishing such gifts that he must fancy I am thinking of dying! But I mean to keep my money and I trust *myself* to squander my inheritance.' Never did a queen have so open-handed a treasurer!

'My lady,' said Hagen of Troneck, 'let me tell you that the King of the Rhenish lands has so much gold and so many clothes to bestow that there is no need for us to take any clothes of yours away with us.'

'I disagree,' replied the Queen. 'Do me the pleasure of letting me fill twenty trunks with silk and gold, so that I may give it away myself when we have crossed over to Gunther's land.' Her coffers were filled with precious stones but they were her own treasurers who had the charge of it, since (much to Gunther's and Hagen's amusement) she was loath to entrust it to Dancwart.

'To whom shall I make over my territories?' asked the Queen. 'Before we leave, you and I must duly appoint a governor.'

'Summon whomever you approve for the office, and we shall constitute him regent,' replied the noble King.

Close at hand the lady saw her maternal uncle, one of her most illustrious kinsmen. 'I hereby commend to you my fortresses and lands,' she told him, 'until such time as Gunther shall have jurisdiction here.' She then chose two thousand of her retainers to sail away with her to Burgundy, in addition to the thousand from Nibelungland. They made ready for the voyage and were seen riding down to the shore. She also took with her eighty-six ladies and at least a hundred maidens, all very comely. And now they lost no time, for they were eager to be gone. But of those whom they were leaving behind them, how many gave way to tears!

Kissing those of her nearest relations who were in attendance, Brunhild decorously left the land that was hers by sovereign right; and, taking a friendly farewell, they gained the open sea. However, the lady never came back to this, her father's country.

As they sailed on, much merrymaking was heard, for they were well supplied with all amusements while an excellent sea-breeze came to speed them on their course, so that it was with great elation that they left the land behind. But Brunhild did not wish to embrace her lord on the way, and so their pleasures were deferred till a high festivity, when, amidst great joy, they and their warriors arrived at Gunther's palace in the castle of Worms.

9

How Siegfried was sent to Worms

When they had voyaged for nine full days, Hagen of Troneck said, 'Listen to what I have to say. We are late with our news to Worms on the Rhine – your messengers should already be in Burgundy.'

'What you say is true,' answered King Gunther, 'and none would serve for the journey as well as yourself, friend Hagen. Now ride home to my country, since none will tell our people better about our visit to the Queen.'

'I am not a good messenger. Let me look after the treasury. I wish to stay on board with the ladies and keep their wardrobe till we have brought them to Burgundy. Ask Siegfried to convey your message, he is the man to carry out this mission with courage and energy. And if he declines to make the journey for you, you must ask him courteously, as a friend, to do it for love of your sister.'

Gunther summoned the hero; and Siegfried came at once when they had found him. 'Since we are nearing home,' said Gunther, 'I should be sending messengers to my dear sister, and to my mother, too, to inform them of our approach. Now I ask you to do this, Siegfried. Carry out my wish and I shall be for ever obliged to you.'
But bold Siegfried refused the good knight's request, till

Gunther earnestly implored him. 'Please ride there for my sake,' he said, 'and for that of comely Kriemhild, so that the noble girl and I will be beholden to you!' Hearing this, brave Siegfried was willingness itself.

'Send whatever messages you please – I shall not fail to impart them. For the sake of the loveliest of maidens I shall gladly discharge your mission. For why should I deny her whom I love so tenderly? Whatever you command in her name shall be done.'

'Then tell my mother Queen Uote that we are in great spirits as a result of our voyage. Inform my brothers of our achievements, and also tell the news to our friends. Do not omit to give my sister, my household and all my retainers a greeting from Brunhild and me, or to say how fully I have attained my heart's desire. And tell my dear nephew Ortwin to have high seats set up at Worms by the Rhine, and let my other kinsmen be advised that, together with Brunhild, I mean to hold a great festivity. Tell my sister further that as soon as she has heard that I have landed with my guests she is to welcome my beloved most attentively, to that I shall never cease to be grateful to her.'

Lord Siegfried with all due form quickly took leave of Brunhild and her suite, and rode towards the Rhenish lands; nor could you have found a better messenger. He rode into Worms accompanied by twenty-four warriors.

[. . .]

'Welcome lord Siegfried, worthy knight!' said noble Kriemhild in kindly greeting. 'But where is my brother, the illustrious King Gunther? We fear that Brunhild's mighty strength may have taken him from us. Alas, that I, poor girl, was ever born!'

'Now give me my reward for good news! You are weeping for no cause, fair ladies. I tell you I left him in good health, and he and Brunhild have sent me to you both with the news. Most noble Queen, Gunther and his beloved send their affectionate greetings. Now let your weeping be, for they will soon be here.'

Not for a long, long time had Kriemhild heard such joyful news. Taking the hem of her snow-white gown, she dabbed at the tears in her pretty eyes; then she thanked the messenger for the news she had received, and her sadness and weeping were no more. She bade her courier be seated – an honour he gladly accepted – and the adorable young woman said to him: 'I should not mind it overmuch if I might give you of my treasure to requite you for your message, but you are too exalted. Instead I shall always be grateful to you.'

'Though I in my one person were lord of thirty lands', he replied, 'I should gladly receive a gift from your hands.'

'Then it shall be done,' said the well-bred girl. And she told her treasurer to go and fetch her guerdon.

Kriemhild repaid her messenger with four-and-twenty bracelets inlaid with fine jewels, but having no mind to keep them the hero at once gave them to her intimates whom he saw there in the chamber. Her mother thanked him most graciously.

'I have news to tell you,' said the warrior, 'of what Gunther would have you do when he arrives in

Burgundy, and for which, my lady, if you do it, he will always be obliged to you. He asks you through me to give his noble guests a kindly welcome, and he begs you to favour him by riding out to meet him on the riverbank by Worms. This, in the loyal affection he bears you, the King bids you do!'

[. . .]

10

How Brunhild was received in Worms

On the far side of the Rhine, the King and his guests, in company after company, could be seen riding towards the riverbank with many maidens led by their escorts, while those who were there to welcome them were in all readiness.

When the Icelanders and Siegfried's men from Nibelungland had boarded the ferries, they plied their oars very actively and made haste to land where the King's friends and relations were assembled on the shore.

And now hear how the noble Queen Uote rode with her maidens from the castle to the river, where numerous knights and young ladies made acquaintance. Duke Gere led Kriemhild's palfrey only to the castle gate, after which it fell to bold Siegfried to escort her, a service for which the lovely girl repaid him well in days to come. Brave Ortwin rode beside Uote, and a host of knights and maidens rode in pairs – never, dare we assert, were so many ladies seen together and at so great a reception!

Many a magnificent bohort was ridden by illustrious knights under the eyes of fair Kriemhild as they progressed towards the boats – an honour which it would have been discourteous to deny her. Then all those well-favoured women were lifted down from their palfreys.

The King had now crossed over together with many noble guests, and what a cracking of stout lances there was to greet the ladies! Shields re-echoed as thrust on thrust was delivered at full tilt, and oh, the din of their fine bosses as these were clashed in the mêlée!

The charming ladies of Burgundy stood there by the harbour as Gunther, leading Brunhild by the hand in person, disembarked with his guests – a refulgence of vivid robes and sparkling gems, each vying with the other!

With great elegance and breeding Kriemhild paced towards Brunhild and her suite, and bade them welcome. They pushed back their fillets, with their gleaming white hands and the two kissed each other as good manners required.

'Welcome to my mother and to me here in this country and to all the loyal friends we have,' said Kriemhild courteously. This Brunhild acknowledged with a bow. The ladies embraced and embraced again, and, indeed, you never heard of a welcome so affectionate as Queen Uote and her daughter extended to the bride, for they kissed her sweet mouth many, many times.

When Brunhild's ladies had all come ashore, handsome knights took fine women by the hand, beyond number, while fair maidens were presented to Brunhild – so that, what with much kissing of red lips, it was long before their greetings were over.

The noble princesses were still standing together, a delight for the eyes of many worthy knights. And those who till then had only heard it asserted that they could never have seen anything so lovely as these two (how well this was proved by the event!) now had them under their scrutiny: and, truly, they detected no fraud in their appearances. Those who were good judges of the charms of the fair praised Gunther's wife for her beauty; but those critics who had looked more discerningly declared Kriemhild to have the advantage.

Women and girls moved forward to meet each other, and very many handsome figures were to be seen there, elegantly robed, against the background of silken tents and magnificent pavilions with which the whole meadow below Worms was filled. Gunther's kinsmen jostled their way through, and inviting Brunhild, Kriemhild, and all the ladies to go into the shade, conducted them to the tents.

But now all the strangers had arrived on their chargers, and they rode many a glorious joust clean through their adversaries' shields, so that the dust began to rise from that plain as though the whole land were on fire. It soon became apparent who were brave warriors! This sport of the knights was watched by many young ladies, and I fancy lord Siegfried rode through the mêlée past the tents in both directions many times. He had brought a thousand fine Nibelungs to the field.

Then, at the King's request, Hagen of Troneck came to part the two sides and bring the bohort to a friendly conclusion lest the pretty girls be all covered with dust, and the guests good-naturedly complied.

'Rest your horses till it begins to grow cool,' said lord Gernot, 'and then let us go jousting up to the great palace in honour of fair ladies. Pray be ready when the King wishes to mount.'

Now that the bohort had ceased throughout the meadow, the knights went to the high pavilions to dally with the ladies in hopes of rare delight, and here they whiled away the time till they had to start for Worms.

At the approach of evening, when the sun was going down and the air was growing cooler, the men and women delayed no longer but repaired to the castle, while the knights' eyes lingered caressingly on the charms of numerous beauties.

And now, after the custom of the land, the good warriors rode their clothes to tatters, all the way up to the palace, where the King dismounted, and then they handed the ladies down, as is ever the way of men of spirit, after which the young Queen and the Princess parted company. For Uote and her daughter entered a vast chamber, together with their suite, and everywhere a merry din arose. High seats were made ready, and the King desired to dine with his guests. Beside him stood fair Brunhild, crowned as a queen of Burgundy, and what a magnificent figure she made! Many benches had been set at fine, broad tables loaded with viands (so the story says), and there was no lack of what was wanted.

Numerous distinguished strangers were seen standing near the King. And now the royal chamberlains brought water for their hands in bowls of red gold, and it would be a waste of effort, since I should not believe it, if someone were to say that better service was given at any princely function. Before the King of the Rhineland dipped his hands, lord Siegfried reminded him, as he was well entitled to do, of the promise which Gunther had given him before he met Brunhild in Iceland.

73

'Remember what you swore to me,' he said, 'namely that when lady Brunhild came to this country you would give me your sister. What has become of your oaths? I went to great trouble on your voyage.'

'It is right that you should remind me,' said the King to his guest. 'I do not intend to forswear myself. I shall help you to achieve your object to the best of my power.'

Kriemhild was summoned before the King, and she appeared at the foot of the hall with her comely maidens in attendance: but at once Giselher leapt down the stair. 'Tell these girls to withdraw – only my sister is to remain with the King!' and so Kriemhild was ushered into the royal presence, where noble knights from many princedoms were standing in the spacious hall. These were bidden to stay where they were, though the lady Brunhild had reached the table.

'Dearest sister,' said King Gunther, 'of your own goodness, redeem my royal oath for me! For I swore to give you to a warrior, and if he becomes your husband you will have done my will most loyally.'

'Do not entreat me, dear brother,' was the noble maiden's answer. 'I shall always be as you wish, and do whatever you command. I shall gladly accept the man whom you give me for a husband, sir.'

Siegfried flushed as her sweet glance rested on him, and then he humbly thanked the lady Kriemhild. Thereupon they were told to stand in the ring together, and she was asked whether she would have the handsome man.

In her maiden modesty she was somewhat abashed, yet Siegfried's luck would have it that she did not reject him there and then, while for his part the noble King of the Netherlands accepted her as his wife.

And now that he had sworn to have her and she him, Siegfried at once took the sweet girl in his arms very tenderly, and kissed his lovely queen in the presence of the warriors.

The suites of both parties dispersed from the ring. Siegfried sat with Kriemhild opposite the King in the high seat of honour to which he had been escorted by a great number of his Nibelungs. The King and the maiden Brunhild now took their seats, and when the latter saw Kriemhild at Siegfried's side – never had she suffered such torment – she began to weep so that the hot tears fell down her radiant cheeks.

'My lady, what is the matter that you allow your bright eyes to be dimmed so?' the sovereign asked. 'You have every cause to rejoice, since my lands, cities, and many fine men are all at your command.'

'I have every cause to weep,' retorted the lovely maiden. 'It wounds me to the heart to see your sister sitting beside a liegeman, and if she is to be degraded in this fashion I shall never cease to lament it!'

'Not another word now,' replied the King. 'I shall tell you some other time why I have given my sister to Siegfried. She has good reason to live happily with the warrior forever.'

'I shall never cease to regret her beauty and fine breeding. How gladly I should take refuge, if only I knew where, so as not to share your couch, unless you were to tell me why Kriemhild should be Siegfried's spouse.'

'I shall tell you plainly,' said the noble King. 'He has

cities and broad lands quite as good as mine, for, rely on it, he is a mighty king! This is why I consent to his loving my fine young beauty.' But Brunhild's heart was troubled, whatever the King said to her.

Then a crowd of worthy knights dashed from the tables, and went at it so hard with their bohort that the whole castle resounded. But in the company of his guests time hung heavy on the King – he fancied it would be pleasanter beside his fair queen, for he was by no means without hope in his heart that she would bring him much delight, and he began to cast amorous glances at her.

The guests were asked to cease from their chivalric sport, since the King wished to retire with his lady. Kriemhild and Brunhild came together at the stairs below the hall, for as yet there was no enmity between them, and were at once joined by their retinues, while their resplendent chamberlains brought lights without delay. Thereupon the two kings' vassals parted company, and many knights escorted Siegfried away.

And now those two great lords had come to where they would lie, and each thought how he would wrest love's victory from his handsome wife, and was comforted in his heart.

Lord Siegfried's pastime was to his vast contentment, for as he lay with the young lady and inured her so tenderly to his noble loves, she became as dear to him as life, and he would not have exchanged her for a thousand others.

But I shall tell you no more of Siegfried's attentions to Kriemhild. Listen instead to how gallant Gunther lay with lady Brunhild – he had lain more pleasantly with other women many a time.

His attendants, both man and woman, had left him. The chamber was quickly barred, and he imagined that he was soon to enjoy her lovely body: but the time when Brunhild would become his wife was certainly not at hand! She went to the bed in a shift of fine white linen, and the noble knight thought to himself: 'Now I have everything here that I ever wished for.' And indeed there was great cause why her beauty should gratify him deeply. He dimmed the lights one after another with his own royal hands, and then, dauntless warrior, he went to the lady. He laid himself close beside her, and with a great rush of joy took the adorable woman in his arms.

He would have lavished caresses and endearments, had the Queen suffered him to do so, but she flew into a rage that deeply shocked him – he had hoped to meet with 'friend', yet what he met was 'foe'!

'Sir,' she said, 'you must give up the thing you have set your hopes on, for it will not come to pass. Take good note of this: I intend to stay a maiden till I have learned the truth about Siegfried.'

Gunther grew very angry with her. He tried to win her by force, and tumbled her shift for her, at which the haughty girl reached for the girdle of stout silk cord that she wore about her waist, and subjected him to great suffering and shame: for in return for being baulked of her sleep, she bound him hand and foot, carried him to a nail, and hung him on the wall. She had put a stop to his love-making! As to him, he all but died, such strength had she exerted.

And now he who had thought to be master began to entreat her. 'Loose my bonds, most noble Queen. I do not fancy I shall ever subdue you, lovely woman, and I shall never again lie so close to you.'

She did not care at all how he fared, since she was lying very snug. He had to stay hanging there the whole night through till dawn, when the bright morning shone through the windows. If Gunther had ever been possessed of any strength, it had dwindled to nothing now.

'Tell me, lord Gunther,' said the handsome maiden, 'would you mind it if your chamberlains were to find you, bound by a woman's hand?'

'It would turn out very ill for you,' answered the noble knight, 'and I should have little honour from it. Now, of your courtesy, let me come to you. Since you object to my embraces so violently, I promise not to lay hands upon your attire.'

The lady then promptly freed him and set him down on his feet – and he then rejoined her in bed. But he lay down at such a distance that he never so much as touched her beautiful gown, nor did she mean to let him bother her.

Their attendants now entered, bringing them new clothes, of which many had been got ready for that morning. But though all were in festive mood, and despite the crown he wore in honour of the day, the lord of the land was dejected.

In fulfilment of the custom, which they dutifully observed, Gunther and Brunhild delayed no longer but went to the minster, where mass was sung. Siegfried appeared there, too, and there was a great press about them.

In accordance with the royal rites, all that they needed by way of crowns and robes had been prepared for their arrival, and they were duly consecrated. This done, all four stood crowned and happy there.

You must know that six hundred or more squires were knighted there in honour of those kings, and great joy arose throughout Burgundy, with much cracking of spear-shafts in the hands of the novices. Comely young ladies were sitting at the windows, and the splendour of many shields shone bright before their eyes. But the King had gone apart from his men and appeared to be in very low spirits, whatever else others might be doing.

Gunther and Siegfried were in very different moods. The latter had divined how the noble warrior felt, and, going up to him, asked: 'Tell me, how did you fare last night?'

'I was utterly humiliated, for I have brought the foul fiend home with me! When I was about to make love to her, she bound me very tight, carried me to a nail, and suspended me high on the wall; and there I hung the whole night through till daybreak, while she lay at her ease – only then did she untie me! I tell you of my misfortune in confidence, as friend to friend.'

'I am truly sorry,' answered mighty Siegfried, 'and I shall prove it, unless my plan offends you. I shall see to it that she lies so close to you tonight that she will never deny you her favours again.' After what he had been through, Gunther's spirits revived at these words. 'This will turn out well for you in the end,' continued lord Siegfried. 'I fancy things went differently for you and me last night; for your sister Kriemhild is dearer to me than life. But lady Brunhild will have to submit to you tonight. I shall enter your room in my magic cloak so secretly that none shall see through my wiles. Send your chamberlains to their quarters. As a sign that I am there and ready to help you I shall put out the lights which the pages will be holding, and then I shall tame your wife for you to enjoy her this night, or lose my life in the attempt.'

'I agree,' replied the King. 'Except that you must not make love to my dear lady in any way. Do anything else you like – even though you killed her, I should find it in my heart to pardon you – for she is a dreadful woman!'

'I promise on my word of honour,' said Siegfried, 'that I shall not make free with her at all. I prefer your lovely sister to any I have ever set eyes on.' And Gunther believed him when he said it.

The knights' sport gave rise to both pleasure and pain! But when the ladies were about to leave for the dining-hall, the bohort with all its uproar was brought to an end, and the chamberlains bade the people make way. Thus the courtyard was emptied of man, woman, and beast, and every lady was escorted to table into the King's presence by a bishop and was followed to the high seats by many stately men.

The King sat there full of happy expectations, with Siegfried's promise ever-present in his mind, so that this one day seemed as long as a month to him; for he could think of nothing else than the enjoyment of his lady. He could scarcely wait for the board to be raised. Then troops of gallant knights appeared before the queens –

fair Brunhild and lady Kriemhild as well, to conduct them to their chambers.

Lord Siegfried sat beside his lovely wife with great affection and delight while her white hands fondled his – when he vanished suddenly before her very eyes! Toying with him thus and then no longer seeing him, the Queen said to her attendants: 'I am amazed! Where can the King have gone? Who took his hands out of mine?' But she did not pursue the matter.

Siegfried had gone to Gunther's chamber where many attendants were standing with lights. These he extinguished in their hands, and Gunther knew that Siegfried was there. He was aware what Siegfried wanted, and dismissed the ladies and maids. This done, the King quickly thrust two stout bolts across, barred the door himself, and hid the lights behind the bed-curtains. And now mighty Siegfried and the fair maiden began a game there was no avoiding and one that gladdened yet saddened the King.

Siegfried laid himself close by the young lady's side. 'Keep away, Gunther, unless you want a taste of the same medicine!' And, indeed, the lady was soon to inflict great hurt on bold Siegfried. But he held his tongue and said not a word. And although Gunther could not see him, he could plainly hear that no intimacies passed between them, for to tell the truth they had very little ease in that bed. Siegfried comported himself as if he were the great King Gunther and clasped the illustrious maiden in his arms – but she flung him out of the bed against a stool nearby so that his head struck it with a mighty crack! Yet the brave man rebounded powerfully, determined to have another try, though when he set about subduing her it cost him very dear – I am sure no woman will ever again so defend herself.

Seeing that he would not desist, the maiden leapt to her feet. 'Stop rumpling my beautiful white shift!' said the handsome girl. 'You are a very vulgar fellow and you shall pay for it dearly – I'll show you!' She locked the rare warrior in her arms and would have laid him in bonds, like the King, so that she might have the comfort of her bed. She took a tremendous revenge on him for having ruffled her clothes. What could his huge strength avail him? She showed him that her might was the greater, for she carried him with irresistible force and rammed him between the wall and a coffer.

'Alas,' thought the hero, 'if I now lose my life to a girl, the whole sex will grow uppish with their husbands for ever after, though they would otherwise never behave so.'

The King heard it all and was afraid for the man; but Siegfried was deeply ashamed and began to lose his temper, so that he fought back with huge strength and closed with Brunhild desperately. To the King it seemed an age before Siegfried overcame her. She gripped his hands so powerfully that the blood spurted from his nails and he was in agony; but it was not long before he forced the arrogant girl to recant the monstrous resolve which she had voiced the night before. Meanwhile nothing was lost on the King, although Siegfried spoke no word. The latter now crushed her on to the bed so violently that she shrieked aloud, such pain did his might inflict on her. Then she groped for the girdle of silk round her waist with intent to bind him, but his hand fought off her attempt so fiercely that her joints cracked all over her body! This settled the issue, and she submitted to Gunther.

'Let me live, noble King!' said she. 'I shall make ample amends for all that I have done to you and shall never again repel your noble advances, since I have found to my cost that you know well how to master a woman.'

Siegfried left the maiden lying there and stepped aside as though to remove his clothes and, without the noble Queen's noticing it, he drew a golden ring from her finger and then took her girdle, a splendid orphrey. I do not know whether it was his pride which made him do it. Later he gave them to his wife, and well did he rue it!

And now Gunther and the lovely girl lay together, and he took his pleasure with her as was his due, so that she had to resign her maiden shame and anger. But from his intimacy she grew somewhat pale, for at love's coming her vast strength fled so that now she was no stronger than any other woman. Gunther had his delight of her lovely body, and had she renewed her resistance what good could it have done her? His loving had reduced her to this.

And now how very tenderly and amorously Brunhild lay beside him till the bright dawn!

Meanwhile Siegfried had gone from the chamber to where a charming lady welcomed him very kindly. He eluded the questions which she was meaning to ask him and long concealed what he had brought for her until she had been crowned in his country, then he did not fail to give what he was destined to bestow on her.

When morning came, the King was in far better spirits than on the day before, so that happiness reigned entire not only among the nobles whom he had invited to his palace and to whom every attention was paid, but also throughout the land.

[. . .]

I I

How Siegfried came home with his queen

When the guests had all departed, Siegfried said to his followers: 'We, too, must make ready to go home.' This was welcome news to his wife. 'When shall we leave?' she asked her husband. 'I do not wish to have to hurry overmuch, because my brothers must first share our lands with me.' This intention of Kriemhild's was unwelcome news to Siegfried.

The three kings came to him and said with one voice: 'Believe us, lord Siegfried, we shall always be ready to serve you truly till we die.' He bowed and thanked them for their kind assurance. 'Furthermore,' added youthful Giselher, 'we mean to share with you the lands and castles that are our sovereign possession, and, jointly with Kriemhild, you shall have your due part of the spacious realms that are subject to us.'

Hearing what those princes had in mind and seeing that they meant it, Siegfried answered them: 'May your hereditary lands and their peoples rest for ever happy, in God's name! Truly, my dear wife can forgo the portion you wished to give her. In the country where she is to be Queen (if I live to see it) she will be richer in possessions than anyone alive. But in whatever else you command I am ready to serve you.'

'You may well renounce my inheritance,' said Lady Kriemhild, 'but it will not be so easy where knights of Burgundy are concerned. They are such as a king may gladly take home to his country and I request my dear brothers to make division of them with me.'

'Take whomever you please,' said lord Gernot. 'You will find many here who will be willing to ride away with you. Of three thousand knights we shall give you a thousand – let them form your household.'

Kriemhild then sent for Hagen of Troneck and Ortwin, to ask them if they and their kinsmen would be her liegemen. But Hagen was incensed. 'Everybody knows that it is not in Gunther's power to give us to anyone!' he cried. 'Let others of your retainers go with you, for the custom of those of Troneck is well known to you. We are bound to abide at court beside the kings and shall continue to serve those whom we have followed hitherto!'

They let the matter rest and made ready to leave. Kriemhild assembled a noble retinue for herself, of thirty-two maidens and five hundred vassals; and Count Ecke-wart, too, went with Siegfried. And now they all took their leave, knights and squires, ladies and maidens, as they were bound to do, and, parting at once with many kisses, cheerfully quitted King Gunther's realm.

Their kinsmen escorted them for a great distance along the roads, and orders were given everywhere throughout the King's territories for their night quarters to be set up at places to their liking. Then messengers were dispatched to Siegmund to inform him and Sieglind that their son and lady Utoe's daughter were on their way from Worms beyond the Rhine, than which no news could be more welcome to them.

'How fortunate I am,' cried Siegmund, 'that I shall have lived to see lovely Kriemhild go crowned in this country! What glory this confers on my inheritance! My noble son Siegfried will have to rule here as king in his own right.' And as reward for this news, Queen Sieglind gave the messenger many lengths of red samite, silver, and heavy gold, so pleased was she to hear it. Their household then attired themselves assiduously, as was fitting.

Learning who were accompanying their son to the Netherlands, the King and Queen at once had high seats erected, and to these, when he was crowned, King Siegfried would go in the presence of his friends.

King Siegmund's vassals rode out to meet Siegfried; and if anyone was ever better received than were those fine warriors in Siegmund's land I have not heard of it. Comely Sieglind rode out to meet Kriemhild with many fair ladies attended by gay knights for a whole day's march, to where the others came in sight. Then natives and strangers alike shared the discomforts of travel together, till they arrived at a great city called Xanten, where the two were afterwards crowned.

With smiling faces (their cares were now over) Siegmund and Sieglind showered affectionate kisses on Kriemhild and Siegfried and gave a hearty welcome to all their followers. The guests were conducted before Siegmund's hall, where the charming young ladies were handed from their palfreys, and there were men in plenty to wait upon these beauties most attentively.

However great the festivity at Worms was held to be, the warriors here in Xanten were given far better clothes than they had worn in all their days. Marvels could be told of the Netherlanders' wealth, as they sat in their glory and abundance. The sight of all the gussets agleam with gold which their followers wore, embroidered on golden wire with pearls and jewels – so well did noble Queen Sieglind care for them!

Then lord Siegmund spoke in the presence of his friends. 'I declare to all of Siegfried's kinsmen that he shall wear my crown, with all these warriors to witness!' – an announcement which delighted the Netherlanders. Then Siegmund made over to his son his crown, his judicature, and his kingdom. From now on Siegfried was their supreme lord. And when any brought a lawsuit before him, and it fell within his jurisdiction, justice was done in such fashion that the son of fair Sieglind was held in great dread.

Siegfried lived thus magnificently and (to tell the truth) dispensed justice as a crowned sovereign until the tenth year, when the lovely lady had a son, thus fulfilling his family's expectations. These hastened to baptize him and gave him the name of Gunther after his maternal uncle, a name he need not be ashamed of. Were he to take after his Burgundian kinsman, things would go well with him. They reared him with care, and had very good reason to do so.

Queen Sieglind died at this time, and Kriemhild now had the entire power which such great ladies are entitled to wield over their territories. Many there were who lamented it that death had taken Sieglind from them.

And (so we are told) fair Brunhild, too, had borne a son to mighty Gunther in Burgundy on the Rhine, and, from affection for the hero, they gave him the name of Siegfried. Noble Gunther commanded that he be watched over most zealously and he appointed tutors who had all the qualities to make an excellent man of him. But – in the end – of how many friends and relations did misfortune rob him!

News was constantly being brought of the splendid life the gay knights were leading in Siegmund's land all this time, and so it was with Gunther and his illustrious family. The land of the Nibelungs was subject to Siegfried in Xanten, as were the warriors of Schilbung, and his and Nibelung's hoard, so that no member of Siegfried's kindred ever had more power, a fact that made his spirits soar the higher. He possessed the greatest treasure ever won by hero, apart from its former owners, and he had gained it in battle at the foot of a mountain thanks to his own strength, slaying many gay knights to get it. He had all the glory that a man can wish for, and even if this had not been the case we should have had to admit that he was one of the best that ever sat on horseback. Many feared his strength of body, and how right they were to do so.

12

How Gunther invited Siegfried to the festival

Now Gunther's queen was thinking, all this time: 'How comes it that lady Kriemhild can carry her head so high while her husband Siegfried is our vassal? It is a long time since he rendered us any dues.' Such were the thoughts which she nursed in her heart, keeping them well hidden, for it vexed her deeply that those two should hold aloof from her and she receive so little service from Siegfried's land; and she longed to know why that should be. Thus she tried to discover from the King whether it might be possible for her to see Kriemhild again and she made her wish known to him in confidence. But her lord did not think too well of her suggestion.

'How can we fetch them here all that way?' asked the mighty King. 'It would not be possible. They live too far away from us for me to venture to invite them.'

'Whatever heights of power a royal vassal might have reached he should not fail to do his sovereign's bidding,' was Brunhild's subtle reply. Gunther smiled at her words, since whenever he saw Siegfried he did not reckon it as homage.

'My dear lord,' she said, 'if you wish to please me, help me to get Siegfried and your sister to visit us – I assure you nothing could make me happier, for what delight it gives me to recall Kriemhild's elegant ways and courteous nature and how we sat together when I first became your wife! Brave Siegfried honours himself in loving her.'

And she kept on begging him, till at last the King said: 'I never saw any guests so gladly as I should see them, believe me. I need very little persuading. I shall dispatch my messengers to them to invite them here to Burgundy.'

'Tell me when you intend to invite them,' said the Queen, 'and when our dear friends are expected here, and let me know whom you mean to send to them.'

'Yes indeed,' replied the King. 'I shall have thirty of my men ride there' – and he immediately summoned them and gave them a message to take to Siegfried's land. Brunhild gave them some very magnificent robes, so pleased was she.

'You warriors are to inform mighty Siegfried and my sister from me – and keep nothing back of what I say – that none could love them more. And ask them both to visit us in our kingdom on the Rhine so that we shall always be obliged to them. Before midsummer he and his followers shall see many here who will hold them in high honour. Give King Siegmund my humble respects, and tell him that my friends and I remain his well-wishers as ever. And ask my sister to be sure to visit her relations, for never was there a festivity that she could more fittingly attend.'

Brunhild and Uote and all the ladies present asked them to deliver their good wishes to the charming noblewomen and all the brave men in Siegfried's country; and with the assent of the royal privy council the messengers set out. They travelled well-equipped for their journey, and when their horses and gear had been brought for them, they quitted the land. Under the protection of the King's safe-conduct, they were in great haste to reach their destination.

After three weeks they rode into Norway, the land to which they had been sent, and there at Nibelung's strong-hold they found the warrior. Their horses were very weary from the long way they had come.

Siegfried and Kriemhild were informed that some knights had arrived wearing clothes after the Burgundian fashion, and the Queen at once rose to her feet from the couch where she was resting and sent a maid to the window. As they stood there in the courtyard, the girl recognized brave Gere and his companions who had been sent to them as messengers, and what glad news it was for Kriemhild's homesick heart!

'See, they are there in the courtyard!' she said to the King. 'Stalwart Gere and his companions, whom my brother Gunther has dispatched down the Rhine to us.'

'They are welcome,' said mighty Siegfried, and the household ran out to them, while each said the kindest things he knew to greet those messengers. Lord Siegmund, too, was very glad of their coming.

Gere and his men were lodged in their quarters and their horses were taken to stable. The envoys were then allowed to present themselves to lord Siegfried and Kriemhild as they sat there side by side, and they accordingly did so. The King and his queen rose immediately and received Gere warmly, together with his comrades, Gunther's men, and then Gere was asked to sit down.

'Allow us to discharge our mission before we take our seats – let your travel-weary visitors remain standing long enough to deliver the message which Gunther and Brunhild, Queen Uote, young Gilselher, lord Gernot and your dearest kinsmen convey to you through us. Their fortunes are flourishing, and they send you their humble compliments from Burgundy!'

'Heaven reward you,' answered Siegfried, 'I well believe their good will and sincerity, as one should where friends are concerned, and the same goes for their sister. Now declare your news and let us know whether our dear friends at home are in good spirits. Tell me, has anyone wronged my wife's relations since we left them? If so, I shall not cease to bear them loyal aid till their enemies have cause to regret my help.'

'They live with undiminished honour and are in excellent spirits. They would be very glad to see you again, never doubt it, and they invite you to the Rhineland to a high festivity. They beg my lady Kriemhild to accompany you and expect you in the spring before midsummer.'

'That would not be easy,' answered mighty Siegfried.

'Your mother Uote, and Gernot and Giselher, have bidden me urge you not to refuse them,' rejoined Gere of Burgundy. 'I have heard them lamenting daily that you live so far away. If it were possible for you to come and see them, Brunhild and all her maidens would be overjoyed to learn it.' This message pleased lovely Kriemhild.

Gere was a near-relation of the Queen's, and the King asked him to be seated; and when Siegfried ordered wine to be poured out for his guests, this was promptly done.

And now Siegmund came and saw the messengers from Burgundy and spoke some friendly words to them. 'Welcome, you knights and vassals of King Gunther! Now that my son Siegfried has taken Kriemhild to wife we ought to see more of you, if you call yourselves our friends.' – To which they answered that they would be glad to come as often as he pleased.

The envoys' hosts banished their weariness with pleasant entertainment. They asked them to sit down, food was set before them, and Siegfried saw to it that his guests had their fill. He prevailed upon them to stay for nine whole days till at last those brave knights began to fret at not being allowed to ride home. Siegfried meanwhile had summoned his friends to ask whether they would advise them to go to the Rhineland or no.

'My good friend Gunther and his kinsmen have sent to invite me to a feast. Now were it not that his country is too far off, I should gladly visit him. They also wish Kriemhild to come with me. Now advise me, dear friends – how can she make the journey there? But had I myself been asked to go campaigning in thirty different countries I could not fail to lend them a helping hand.'

'If you have a mind to go and attend the festivity,' replied his knights, 'we shall tell you what you should do. You must ride to the Rhenish lands with a thousand warriors, then you can stay in Burgundy with honour.'

'If you are going to the festivity why don't you inform *me*?' asked lord Siegmund of the Netherlands. 'I shall ride with you, if you have nothing against it. I shall take a hundred knights with me and so swell the ranks of your party.'

'I shall be glad if you are coming with us, dear father,' answered Siegfried. 'I shall be leaving in twelve days' time,' – and all who asked were given horses and clothes.

Now that the noble King had decided to make the journey the brave envoys were told to return. Through them, Siegfried sent a message to Burgundy informing his wife's relations that he would be delighted to join them at their feast. We are told that both Siegfried and Kriemhild bestowed so many gifts on the envoys that their mounts could not carry it all home, so wealthy a king was he – hence they jubilantly drove sturdy pack-horses away with them!

Siegfried and Siegmund furnished clothes for their followers, and Count Eckewart at once had the whole land scoured for the finest ladies' gowns that could be got hold of anywhere. Saddles and shields were made ready, and the knights and ladies who were to accompany Siegfried and Kriemhild were given what they needed so that they should want for nothing. Siegfried was taking many distinguished guests to see his friends.

The envoys made great speed over the roads that took them homewards, and when at last brave Gere arrived in Burgundy and they all dismounted before Gunther's hall, he was very well received. Both young and old came to ask for news (as they always do), but the good knight said to them, 'You will hear it when I tell the King,' and went in with his companions to Gunther.

The King leapt up from his throne for sheer pleasure,

and fair Brunhild thanked them for having come so soon. 'How is Siegfried, who was so kind to me?' Gunther asked his envoys.

'Both he and your sister flushed red for joy. No man of any condition ever sent his friends such loyal greetings as lord Siegfried and his father have sent you.'

'Tell me, is Kriemhild coming?' the Queen asked the Margrave. 'Does she retain the elegant style that used to be all her own?'

'She is most assuredly coming to see you,' was Gere's answer.

Then Uote quickly summoned the messengers, and you could easily tell from the way she asked that she was eager to learn how Kriemhild was. Gere told Uote how he had found her, and said she would be coming soon.

Nor did the envoys fail to tell the court of the gifts that lord Siegfried had made them. Thus the gold and the robes were fetched so that they could be displayed before the three kings' vassals, earning grateful applause for Siegfried's and Kriemhild's munificence.

'It is easy for him to bestow gifts,' said Hagen. 'Were he to live for ever he could never squander all that he owns, for he holds the Nibelungs' hoard in his power. Ah me, if that were to come to Burgundy!'

The household lived in joyful expectation of their coming. Morning and evening the kings' retainers knew no rest as they erected countless seats, while bold Hunold and brave Sindold, aided by Ortwin, were busy directing butlers and stewards to set the benches up. For this Gunther thanked them all.

And how well Rumold, Lord of the Kitchen, governed his subjects, the great cauldrons, pots and pans! What multitudes there were of them, as the viands were made ready for the guests!

13

How Siegfried went to the festival with his queen

Let us leave all their bustle and tell how Kriemhild and her maidens journeyed from the land of the Nibelungs and on towards the Rhine.

Numerous coffers were got ready for the sumpters to take the road, and no horses ever carried fine robes in such number. And now brave Siegfried and his queen set out with their friends for where they were expecting much joy, though it turned out to the great sorrow of them all.

Siegfried and Kriemhild left their little son at home, since there was nothing else they could do. Great trouble arose for him from their visit to Worms, for he never saw his parents again.

Lord Siegmund rode off with them, too. But had he realized how things were to fall out later at the festivity he would not have attended it, since no greater affliction could have befallen him through those who were so dear to him.

They sent messengers ahead of them to tell the Burgundians they were coming, and accordingly many of Uote's friends and Gunther's vassals rode out to meet them, a delightful company, while the King himself made strenuous preparations for receiving his guests.

Going to where Brunhild was sitting, Gunther asked her: 'Do you remember how my sister welcomed you when you entered my country? Please receive Siegfried's queen with the same honours.'

'I shall most willingly,' she answered, 'for I wish her well, as she deserves.'

'They will be arriving tomorrow morning. If you mean to give them a welcome you must bestir yourself so as not to receive them here in the castle, for never have I been visited by such very dear guests.'

Brunhild at once asked her ladies and maids to seek out the best clothes they had, to wear before their guests, and it goes without saying that they needed no prompting. Gunther's men, too, were quick to wait on them with their palfreys. Gunther then assembled all his warriors and the Queen rode out with great magnificence.

They received their dear guests with many salutations and indescribable joy, and people thought that even lady Kriemhild had not welcomed Queen Brunhild so warmly.

Those who had never seen Kriemhild before now learnt how beauty can fire a man. Meanwhile Siegfried had arrived with his men, and you could see them winding to and fro all over the meadow in vast companies, so that there was no avoiding the press and the dust.

When the lord of the land saw Siegfried and Siegmund, he said affectionately: 'You are very welcome indeed to me and all my friends, and we are happy and proud at your coming.'

'May Heaven repay you,' answered Siegmund, the ever-eager in pursuit of honour. 'Ever since my son Siegfried gained your friendship I have felt an urge to meet you.'

'I am very glad you came,' replied King Gunther.

With the courteous participation of Gernot and Giselher, Siegfried was welcomed with all the honours due to him and none bore him a grudge. I fancy no guests ever had better treatment.

The two queens now approached each other, and many saddles were emptied as the knights lifted whole bevies of fine-looking women down on to the grass; for there was a great flurry about them of those who liked waiting on ladies. Thereupon that lovely pair went up to each other, and it was a joy to countless knights that they greeted each other so courteously. Warriors were standing there in crowds beside the queens' maidens, and now the knights and the young ladies took one another's hands, and there was much elegant bowing and sweet kissing by those fair ones, a spectacle that delighted the men of both Gunther and Siegfried.

They delayed no longer but rode up to the town, and the King asked his people to make it plain to his guests that they were very glad to see them in Burgundy. Thus they rode many splendid jousts under the eyes of the young ladies. Here Hagen of Troneck and Ortwin showed their authority, since none dared flout their commands, and much honour was paid to the visitors – under the thrusts and charges countless shields resounded all the way up to the castle gate, and the King himself halted outside for a long time with his guests before he entered, so pleasantly did they while away the hour.

But now they rode up to the broad palace in high spirits, and, flowing down from fair ladies' saddles, many fine brocades, well cut and ingeniously woven, caught the eye on all sides. Gunther's attendants appeared at once, and he told them to take the guests to their chambers. Now and again Brunhild darted a glance at lady Kriemhild who looked so very lovely, the radiance of her fair face vying magnificently with its setting of gold.

The hubbub of Siegfried's retinue could be heard all over the city of Worms. Gunther asked his marshal Dancwart to see to their needs, and Dancwart accordingly set about finding agreeable quarters for them. He ordered food to be brought for them, both within and without the fortress, and visitors from abroad never received better attention: whatever they desired was given them – the King was so rich that nobody was denied anything and they were served with the utmost good will.

The King sat down with his guests. Siegfried was asked to sit at the same seat as before, and as he went to take it he was attended by many splendid knights. Fully twelve hundred warriors sat at table in his ring, and Queen Brunhild was thinking no liege man could ever be mightier. Her feelings towards him were still friendly enough for her to let him live.

That evening, while the King sat and dined, many fine robes were splashed with wine as the butlers plied the tables – they served the guests eagerly and plentifully, as has long been the custom at feasts. The King gave orders for the ladies and maidens to be comfortably lodged: he wished to serve them wherever they came from, and they all had to receive his bounty as a sign of his esteem.

When the night came to an end and dawn appeared, the ladies opened their coffers, and the lustre of innumerable jewels shone out from the fine stuffs as their hands moved among them, choosing many splendid robes. But while it was not yet full daylight, a host of knights and squires arrived before the hall, and once again the tumult was heard as young warriors jousted so spiritedly that, before early matins were sung for the King, they had earned his commendation! The crack of many trumpets rang out loud and clear, and the sound of drums and flutes grew so great that spacious Worms re-echoed with it, a sign for proud warriors everywhere to leap into their saddles.

And now far and wide and in great number the good knights began a most noble sport: you could see many there whose youthful hearts fired them with great zest, all fine, gallant knights beneath their shields! Magnificent women and bevies of lovely girls adorned in all their finery sat in the windows watching the pastime of all those fearless men, till the King and his friends took the field. Thus they passed the time, which did not lie heavy on their hands, till the bells pealed from the minster. The queens' and their ladies' palfreys were fetched and they all rode off, attended by troops of knights. When they arrived before the cathedral they dismounted on the grass. Brunhild was as yet well disposed towards her guests, and they all entered together in their crowns.

Nevertheless, as a result of a bitter quarrel their friendship was soon to be broken.

When they had heard mass they returned, and with much ceremony went happily to table. Nor did their joy at that high feast droop till the eleventh day.

14

How the queens railed at each other

Before vespers one evening there arose in the courtyard a great turmoil of warriors pursuing their pleasure at their knightly sports, and a crowd of men and women ran up to watch.

The mighty queens had sat down together, and their thoughts were on two splendid knights.

'I have a husband of such merit that he might rule over all the kingdoms of this region,' said fair Kriemhild.

'How could that be?' asked lady Brunhild. 'If there were no others alive but you and he, all these kingdoms might well subserve him, but as long as Gunther lives it could never come about.'

'See how magnificently he bears himself, and with what splendour he stands out from the other knights, like the moon against the stars,' rejoined Kriemhild. 'It is not for nothing that I am so happy.'

'However splendid and handsome and valiant your husband may be,' replied Brunhild, 'you must nevertheless give your noble brother the advantage. Let me tell you truly: Gunther must take precedence over all kings.'

'My husband is a man of such worth,' answered lady Kriemhild, 'that I have not praised him vainly. His honour stands high on very many counts. Believe me, Brunhild, he is fully Gunther's equal.'

'Now do not misunderstand me, Kriemhild, for I did not speak without cause. When I saw them for the first time and the King subdued me to his will and won my love so gallantly, I heard them both declare – and Siegfried himself said so – that he was Gunther's vassal, and so I consider him to be my liegeman, having heard him say so.'

'It would be a sad thing for me if that were so,' retorted Kriemhild. 'How could my noble brothers have had a hand in my marrying a liegeman? I must ask you in all friendship, Brunhild, if you care for me, kindly to stop saying such things.'

'I cannot,' answered the Queen, 'for why should I renounce my claim to so many knights who owe us service through Siegfried?'

At this lovely Kriemhild lost her temper. 'You will have to renounce your claim to him and to his attending you with services of any kind! He ranks above my noble brother Gunther, and you must spare me such things as I have had to hear. I must say I find it very odd, since he is your liegeman and you have such power over us, that he has been sitting on his dues for so long! You should not bother me with your airs.'

'You are getting above yourself,' replied the Queen, 'and I should like to see whether you are held in such esteem as I.' The ladies were growing very angry.

'We shall very soon see!' said lady Kriemhild. 'Since you have declared my husband to be your liegeman, the two kings' vassals must witness today whether I dare enter the minster before the Queen of the land. You must see visible proof this day that I am a free noblewoman, and that my husband is a better man than yours. Nor do I intend for my part to be demeaned by what you say. You shall see this evening how your liegewoman will walk in state in Burgundy in sight of the warriors. I claim to be of higher station than was ever heard of concerning any queen that wore a crown!' And now indeed fierce hate grew up between those ladies.

'If you deny you are a vassal, you and your ladies must withdraw from my suite when we enter the cathedral.'

'We certainly shall,' answered Kriemhild. 'Now dress yourselves well, my maidens,' she said to them, 'for I must not be put to shame. Let it appear beyond all doubt whether you have fine clothes or not. We must make Brunhild eat her words.'

They needed little persuading and fetched out their sumptuous robes. And when all the ladies and maidens were beautifully attired, Queen Kriemhild, herself exquisitely gowned, set out with her train of forty-three maids-in-waiting whom she had brought with her to Worms, all dressed in dazzling cloth-of-gold from Arabia.

And so those shapely girls arrived at the minster, before which Siegfried's men were waiting, so that people were wondering why it was that the queens appeared separately and no longer went together as before. However, in the end, many brave knights had to suffer dearly for their division.

Gunther's queen was already standing before the cathedral and all the knights were passing the time pleasantly taking note of her lovely women, when lady Kriemhild arrived with a great and splendid company. However fine the clothes ever worn by daughters of any noble knights, they were as nothing beside those of her suite: Kriemhild was so rich in possessions that thirty queens could not have found the wherewithal to do as she had done. Even if his wishes were to come true, no man could assert that he had ever seen such magnificent clothes paraded as Kriemhild's fair maidens were wearing, though she would not have demanded it except to spite Brunhild.

The two processions met before the minster and the lady of the land, prompted by great malice, harshly ordered Kriemhild to halt. 'A liegewoman may not enter before a queen!'

'It would have been better for you if you could have held your tongue,' said fair Kriemhild angrily, 'for you have brought dishonour on your own pretty head. How could a vassal's paramour ever wed a king?'

'Whom are you calling a paramour?' asked the Queen.

'I call you one,' answered Kriemhild. 'My dear husband Siegfried was the first to enjoy your lovely body, since it was not my brother who took your maidenhead. Where were your poor wits? – It was a vile trick. – Seeing that he is your vassal, why did you let him love you? Your complaints have no foundation.'

'I swear I shall tell Gunther of this,' replied Brunhild.

'What is that to me? Your arrogance has got the better of you. You used words that made me your servant, and, believe me, in all sincerity I shall always be sorry you did so. I can no longer keep your secrets.'

Brunhild began to weep, and Kriemhild delayed no more but, accompanied by her train, entered the cathedral before Gunther's queen. Thus great hatred arose and bright eyes grew very moist and dim from it.

However pious the ministrations and the chanting, the service seemed to Brunhild as though it would never end, since she was troubled to the depths of her being. Many good warriors had to pay for it later. At last she went out with her ladies and took her stand before the minster thinking: 'Kriemhild must tell me more about this thing of which she accuses me so loudly, sharp-tongued woman that she is. If Siegfried has boasted of it, it will cost him his life!'

And now noble Kriemhild appeared, attended by many brave knights. 'Halt for one moment,' said lady Brunhild. 'You declared me to be a paramour – now prove it! Let me tell you, your remarks have offended me deeply.'

'You would do better not to stand in my way! I prove it with this gold ring on my finger here which my sweetheart brought me when he first slept with you.' Never had Brunhild known a day so fraught with pain.

'This noble ring was stolen and has long been maliciously withheld from me! But now I shall get to the bottom of this affair and discover who took it.' The two ladies were now very agitated.

'You shall not make me the thief who stole it! If you cared for your honour it would have been wise to hold your tongue. As proof that I am not lying, see this girdle which I have round me – you shared my Siegfried's bed!' She was wearing a fine silk braid from Nineveh adorned with precious stones, and Brunhild burst into tears when she saw it. She was resolved that Gunther should hear of this, together with the men of Burgundy. 'Ask the lord of the Rhenish lands to come here. I want to tell him how his sister has insulted me; for she openly declares me to be Siegfried's concubine.'

The King came with his warriors and saw his spouse in tears. 'Tell me, dear lady,' he said very tenderly, 'has anyone annoyed you?'

'I have cause enough to be unhappy. Your sister means to rob me of my honour. I accuse her before you of having said for all to hear that her husband made me his paramour!'

'She would have acted very ill if she had,' said King Gunther.

'She is wearing the girdle that I lost and my ring of red gold. I shall regret the day that I was born unless you clear me of this monstrous infamy, Sire, and earn my eternal thanks!'

'Ask Siegfried to appear. The knight from the Netherlands must either tell us that he made this boast or deny it.' And Kriemhild's beloved husband was summoned at once.

When lord Siegfried saw the queens' distress (he had no idea what was amiss) he quickly asked: 'Why are these ladies weeping? I should very much like to know. Or why has the King sent for me?'

'I deeply regret this necessity,' said King Gunther, 'but my lady Brunhild tells me some tale of your having boasted you were the first to enjoy her lovely person – so your wife, lady Kriemhild, avers.'

'If she said this,' answered mighty Siegfried, 'she will regret it before I have finished with her. I am willing in the presence of your vassals to rebut with my most solemn oaths that I ever said this to her.'

'You must give us proof of that. If the oath you offer is duly sworn here I shall clear you of all treason.' And he commanded the proud Burgundians to stand in a ring. Brave Siegfried raised his hand to swear but the mighty King said: 'Your great innocence is so well known to me that I acquit you of my sister's allegation and accept that you are not guilty of the deed.'

'If my wife were to go unpunished for having distressed Brunhild I should be extremely sorry, I assure you,' rejoined Siegfried, at which the good knights exchanged meaningful glances. 'Women should be trained to avoid irresponsible chatter,' continued Siegfried. 'Forbid your wife to indulge in it, and I shall do the same with mine. I am truly ashamed at her unseemly behaviour.'

All those comely women parted in silence. But Brunhild was so dejected that Gunther's vassals could not but pity her. Then Hagen of Troneck came to his liege lady, and, finding her in tears, asked her what was vexing her. She told him what had happened, and he at once vowed that Kriemhild's man should pay for it, else Hagen, because of that insult, would never be happy again. Then Ortwin and Gernot arrived where the knights were plotting Siegfried's death and took part in their discussion. Noble Uote's son Giselher came next, and, hearing their deliberations, he asked in his loyal-hearted fashion: 'Why are you doing this, good knights? Siegfried has never in any way deserved such hatred that he should die for it. Why, it is a trifle over which the women are quarrelling!'

'Are we to rear cuckoos?' asked Hagen. 'That would bring small honour to such worthy knights. His boast that he enjoyed my dear lady shall cost him his life, or I shall die avenging it!'

'He has done us nothing but good,' interposed the King himself, 'and he has brought us honour. He must be allowed to live. To what purpose should I now turn against him? – He has always shown us heartfelt loyalty.'

'His great strength shall not avail him,' said brave Ortwin of Metz. 'If my lord will let me, I shall do him some harm!'

Thus those warriors declared themselves his enemies, though he had done them no wrong. Yet none followed Ortwin's proposal, except that Hagen kept putting it to Gunther that if Siegfried were no more, Gunther would be lord of many kingdoms, at which Gunther grew very despondent.

There they let the matter rest and went to look at the sports. And what a forest of stout shafts was shattered before the minster and all the way up to the hall for Kriemhild to see! But, for their part, many of Gunther's men nursed feelings of resentment.

'Let your murderous anger be,' said the King. 'Siegfried was born for our honour and good fortune, and moreover he is so terribly strong and so prodigiously brave that were he to get wind of it, none could dare oppose him.'

'He will not,' answered Hagen. 'You just say nothing at all, and I fancy I shall manage this so well in secret that he will repent of Brunhild's weeping. I declare that I, Hagen, shall always be his enemy!'

'How could the thing be done?' asked King Gunther.

'I will tell you,' replied Hagen. 'We shall send envoys to ourselves here in Burgundy to declare war on us publicly, men whom no one knows. Then you will announce in the hearing of your guests that you and your men plan to go campaigning, whereupon Siegfried will promise you his aid, and so he will lose his life. For in this way I shall learn the brave man's secret from his wife.'

The King followed his vassal Hagen's advice, to evil effect, and those rare knights began to set afoot the great betrayal before any might discover it, so that, thanks to the wrangling of two women, countless warriors met their doom.

15

How Siegfried was betrayed

Four days later, in the morning, thirty-two men were seen riding to court who were to tell mighty Gunther that war had been declared on him – a lie from which ladies were to reap the greatest sorrow.

The envoys received permission to go before the King and they announced that they were men of that same Liudeger whom in time past Siegfried had overcome and brought captive to Gunther's country. The King greeted them and bade them go and sit down, but one of their number replied: 'Sire, allow us to stand till we have delivered the message which has been sent to you; for you must know that you have many a mother's son for your enemy. Liudegast and Liudeger, on whom you once inflicted fearful hurt, declare themselves at war with you and intend to invade you with their army here in Burgundy.'

The King was incensed at this news and ordered these accomplices in treachery to their quarters. How could lord Siegfried or anyone else save himself from their plotting – plotting that fell out to their own torment in the end?

Gunther went conversing with his friends in whispers, and Hagen of Troneck would not let him rest – a number of the King's friends would have composed the affair even now at this late hour – but Hagen would not give up his plot.

One day, Siegfried found them with their heads together and asked them: 'Why are the King and his men so dejected? I shall always help to avenge him if anyone has wronged him.'

'I have good reason to be downcast,' answered lord Gunther, 'for Liudegast and Liudeger have declared war on me. They intend to invade me openly.'

'I, Siegfried, shall prevent it with all energy, as befits your honour, and I will deal with them now as I dealt with them before. I shall lay waste their lands and castles before I have finished with them, let my head be your pledge for it! You and your warriors must stay at home and let me ride against them with the men that I have here. I shall show you how glad I am to help you. Believe me, I shall make your enemies suffer!'

'How your words hearten me,' answered the King, as though he were seriously pleased at Siegfried's help. And the faithless man in his perfidy thanked him with a low bow.

'Have no fear,' said lord Siegfried.

Then, in a way that Siegfried and his men were bound to see, they prepared for the expedition with their squires, and Siegfried in turn told his Netherlanders to make ready, and they accordingly fetched out their armour.

'My father Siegmund, please remain here. If Heaven proves kind we shall be returning to the Rhineland shortly. You stay here with the King and enjoy yourself.'

They tied on their standards as though about to leave,

and there were many of Gunther's men who did not know the reason. A great crowd of followers could be seen about Siegfried and they bound their helmets and corselets on to their mounts as many strong knights prepared to quit Burgundy.

Then Hagen of Troneck went to Kriemhild and asked for leave to depart, saying they were going abroad.

'How fortunate I am,' she replied, 'that I have a husband who has the courage to protect my dear relations as my lord Siegfried does. This makes me very happy. My dear friend, Hagen,' continued the Queen, 'bear it in mind that I am always ready to serve you and have never borne you any ill will, so let me have the benefit of it where my dear husband is concerned – he must not be made to pay for any wrong that I may have done to Brunhild. I have since repented of my fault, and Siegfried has beaten me soundly and taken ample vengeance for my having said anything that vexed her.'

'You and she are bound to be reconciled as the days go by,' he answered. 'Now tell me, Kriemhild, dear lady, what can I do for you with regard to your husband Siegfried? I should do it willingly, since there is none towards whom I am better disposed than you, ma'am.'

'I should not be afraid of anyone killing him in battle,' replied the noble lady, 'if only he would not let his rashness get the better of him. Apart from that, the good warrior would never come to harm.'

'My lady,' said Hagen, 'if you have any apprehension that a weapon might wound him tell me by what means I can prevent it, and I shall always guard him, riding or walking.'

'You and I are of one blood, dear Hagen, and I earnestly commend my beloved spouse to you to guard him.' Then she divulged some matters that had better been left alone. 'My husband is very brave and very strong,' she said. 'When he slew the dragon at the foot of the mountain the gallant knight bathed in its blood, as a result of which no weapon has pierced him in battle ever since. Nevertheless, when he is at the wars in the midst of all the javelins that warriors hurl, I fear I may lose my dear husband. Alas, how often do I not suffer cruelly in my fear for Siegfried! Now I shall reveal this to you in confidence, dearest kinsman, so that you may keep faith with me, and I shall tell you, trusting utterly in you, where my dear husband can be harmed. When the hot blood flowed from the dragon's wound and the good knight was bathing in it, a broad leaf fell from the linden between his shoulder-blades. It is there that he can be wounded, and this is why I am so anxious.'

'Sew a little mark on his clothing so that I shall know where I must shield him in battle.' She fancied she was saving the hero, yet this was aimed at his death.

'I will take some fine silk and sew on a cross that none will notice,' she said, 'and there, knight, you must shield him when the battle is joined, and he faces his foes in the onrush.'

'I shall indeed, my dear lady.' – And she fondly imagined that it was for Siegfried's good, though her husband was betrayed by it. Hagen took his leave and went away rejoicing.

The King's followers were all in great heart. I fancy no warrior will ever again perpetrate such treachery as

Hagen contrived, when Queen Kriemhild put her trust in him.

The next morning, lord Siegfried set out happily with a thousand of his men, imagining he would avenge his friends' wrongs, while Hagen rode near enough to be able to survey his clothes. And when Hagen had observed the mark he secretly dispatched two of his men to report news of a different sort – that Liudeger had sent them to King Gunther to say that Burgundy would be left at peace. How loath Siegfried was to ride home again without striking a blow for his friends – Gunther's men could scarcely get him to turn about!

When Siegfried rode back to the King, the latter thanked him: 'May Heaven reward you for your good intentions, friend Siegfried, and for being so ready to meet my wishes. I shall always seek to repay you, as I am bound to do, and put my trust in you before all my friends. But now that we have been spared this campaign I intend to go hunting the bear and the boar in the forest of the Vosges, as I have so often done.' It was the traitor Hagen who had put him up to this.

'Announce it to all my guests that we shall ride out very early and that those who wish to hunt with me are to make their preparations, but that those others have my blessing who wish to stay and wait on the ladies.'

'If you are riding out hunting,' said lord Siegfried generously, 'I shall be glad to accompany you. If you will lend me a tracker and some hounds I will ride into the forest.'

'Do you wish to take only one?' asked the King immediately. 'If you like, I will lend you four that have intimate knowledge of the forest and of the paths which the game follows and who will not lose the scent and send you home empty-handed.'

Then gallant Siegfried rode off to his wife, and Hagen quickly told the King how he planned to get the better of him.

Never should a man practise such monstrous treachery.

16

How Siegfried was slain

The fearless warriors Gunther and Hagen treacherously proclaimed a hunt in the forest where they wished to chase the boar, the bear, and the bison – and what could be more daring? Siegfried rode with their party in magnificent style. They took all manner of food with them; and it was while drinking from a cool stream that the hero was to lose his life at the instigation of Brunhild, King Gunther's queen.

Bold Siegfried went to Kriemhild while his and his companions' hunting-gear was being loaded on to the sumpters in readiness to cross the Rhine, and she could not have been more afflicted. 'God grant that I may see you well again, my lady,' he said, kissing his dear wife, 'and that your eyes may see me too. Pass the time pleasantly with your relations who are so kind to you, since I cannot stay with you at home.'

Kriemhild thought of what she had told Hagen, but she dared not mention it and began to lament that she had ever been born. 'I dreamt last night – and an ill-omened dream it was –' said lord Siegfried's noble queen, weeping with unrestrained passion, 'that two boars chased you over the heath and the flowers were dyed with blood! How can I help weeping so? I stand in great dread of some attempt against your life. – What if we have offended any men who have the power to vent their malice on us? Stay away, my lord, I urge you.'

'I shall return in a few days time, my darling. I know of no people here who bear me any hatred. Your kinsmen without exception wish me well, nor have I deserved otherwise of them.'

'It is not so, lord Siegfried. I fear you will come to grief. Last night I had a sinister dream of how two mountains fell upon you and hid you from my sight! I shall suffer cruelly if you go away and leave me.' But he clasped the noble woman in his arms and after kissing and caressing her fair person very tenderly, took his leave and went forthwith. Alas, she was never to see him alive again.

They rode away deep into the forest in pursuit of their sport. Gunther and his men were accompanied by numbers of brave knights, but Gernot and Giselher stayed at home. Ahead of the hunt many horses had crossed the Rhine laden with their bread, wine, meat, fish, and various other provisions such as a king of Gunther's wealth is bound to have with him.

The proud and intrepid hunters were told to set up their lodges on a spacious isle in the river on which they were to hunt, at the skirt of the greenwood over towards the spot where the game would have to break cover. Siegfried, too, had arrived there, and this was reported to the King. Thereupon the sportsmen everywhere manned their relays.

'Who is going to guide us through the forest to our quarry, brave warriors?' asked mighty Siegfried.

'Shall we split up before we start hunting here?' asked

Hagen. 'Then my lords and I could tell who are the best hunters on this foray into the woods. Let us share the huntsmen men and hounds between us and each take the direction he likes – and then all honour to him that hunts best!' At this, the hunters quickly dispersed.

'I do not need any hounds,' said lord Siegfried, 'except for one tracker so well fleshed that he recognizes the tracks which the game leave through the wood: then we shall not fail to find our quarry.'

An old huntsman took a good sleuth-hound and quickly led the lord to where there was game in abundance. The party chased everything that was roused from its lair, as good hunting-men still do today. Bold Siegfried of the Netherlands killed every beast that his hound started, for his hunter was so swift that nothing could elude him. Thus, versatile as he was, Siegfried outshone all the others in that hunt.

The very first kill was when he brought down a strong young tusker, after which he soon chanced on an enormous lion. When his hound had roused it he laid a keen arrow to his bow and shot it so that it dropped in its tracks at the third bound. Siegfried's fellow-huntsmen acclaimed him for this shot. Next, in swift succession, he killed a wisent, an elk, four mighty aurochs, and a fierce and monstrous buck – so well mounted was he that nothing, be it hart or hind, could evade him. His hound then came upon a great boar, and, as this turned to flee, the champion hunter at once blocked his path, bringing him to bay; and when in a trice the beast sprang at the hero in a fury, Siegfried slew him with his sword, a feat no other hunter could have performed with such ease.

After the felling of this boar, the tracker was returned to his leash and Siegfried's splendid bag was made known to the Burgundians.

'If it is not asking too much, lord Seigfried,' said his companions of the chase, 'do leave some of the game alive for us. You are emptying the hills and woods for us today.' At this the brave knight had to smile.

There now arose a great shouting of men and clamour of hounds on all sides, and the tumult grew so great that the hills and the forest re-echoed with it – the huntsmen had unleashed no fewer than four and twenty packs! Thus, many beasts had to lose their lives there, since each of these hunters was hoping to bring it about that *he* should be given the high honours of the chase. But when mighty Siegfried appeared beside the camp-fire there was no chance of that.

The hunt was over, yet not entirely so. Those who wished to go to the fire brought the hides of innumerable beasts, and game in plenty – what loads of it they carried back to the kitchen to the royal retainers! And now the noble King had it announced to those fine hunters that he wished to take his repast, and there was one great blast of the horn to tell them that he was back in camp.

At this, one of Siegfried's huntsmen said: 'Sir, I have heard a horn-blast telling us to return to our lodges. – I shall answer it.' There was much blowing to summon the companions.

'Let us quit the forest, too,' said lord Siegfried. His mount carried him at an even pace, and the others hastened away with him but with the noise of their going they started a savage bear, a very fierce beast.

'I shall give our party some good entertainment,' he said over his shoulder. 'Loose the hound, for I can see a bear which will have to come back to our lodges with us. It will not be able to save itself unless it runs very fast.' The hound was unleashed, and the bear made off at speed. Siegfried meant to ride it down but soon found that his way was blocked and his intention thwarted, while the mighty beast fancied it would escape from its pursuer. But the proud knight leapt from his horse and started to chase it on foot, and the animal, quite off its guard, failed to elude him. And so he quickly caught and bound it, without having wounded it at all – nor could the beast use either claws or teeth on the man. Siegfried tied it to his saddle, mounted his horse, and in his high-spirited fashion led it to the camp-fire in order to amuse the good knights.

And in what magnificent style Siegfried rode! He bore a great spear, stout of shaft and broad of head; his handsome sword reached down to his spurs; and the fine horn which this lord carried was of the reddest gold. Nor have I ever heard tell of a better hunting outfit: he wore a surcoat of costly black silk and a splendid hat of sable, and you should have seen the gorgeous silken tassels on his quiver, which was covered in panther-skin for the sake of its fragrant odour! He also bore a bow so strong that apart from Siegfried any who wished to span it would have had to use a rack. His hunting suit was all of otter-skin, varied throughout its length with furs of other kinds from whose shining hair clasps of gold gleamed out on either side of this daring lord of the hunt. The handsome sword that he wore was Balmung, a weapon so keen and with such excellent edges that it never failed to bite when swung against a helmet. No wonder this splendid hunter was proud and gay. And (since I am bound to tell you all) know that his quiver was full of good arrows with gold mountings and heads a span in width, so that any beast they pierced must inevitably soon die.

Thus the noble knight rode along, the very image of a hunting man. Gunther's attendants saw him coming and ran to meet him to take his horse – tied to whose saddle he led a might bear! On dismounting, he loosed the bonds from its muzzle and paws, whereupon all the hounds that saw it instantly gave tongue. The beast made for the forest and the people were seized with panic. Affrighted by the tumult, the bear strayed into the kitchen – and how the cooks scuttled from their fire at its approach! Many cauldrons were sent flying and many fires were scattered, while heaps of good food lay among the ashes. Lords and retainers leapt from their seats, the bear became infuriated, and the King ordered all the hounds on their leashes to be loosed – and if all had ended well they would have had a jolly day! Bows and spears were no longer left idle, for the brave ones ran towards the bear, yet there were so many hounds in the way that none dared shoot. With the whole mountain thundering with people's cries the bear took to flight before the hounds and none could keep up with it but Siegfried, who ran it down and then dispatched it with his sword. The bear was later carried to the camp-fire, and all who had witnessed this feat declared that Siegfried was a very powerful man.

The proud companions were then summoned to table. There were a great many seated in that meadow. Piles of sumptuous dishes were set before the noble huntsmen, but the butlers who were to pour their wine were very slow to appear. Yet knights could not be better cared for than they and if only no treachery had been lurking in their minds those warriors would have been above reproach.

'Seeing that we are being treated to such a variety of dishes from the kitchen,' said lord Siegfried, 'I fail to understand why the butlers bring us no wine. Unless we hunters are better looked after, I'll not be a companion of the hunt. I thought I had deserved better attention.'

'We shall be very glad to make amends to you for our present lack,' answered the perfidious King from his table. 'This is Hagen's fault – he wants us to die of thirst.'

'My very dear lord,' replied Hagen of Troneck, 'I thought the day's hunting would be away in the Spessart and so I sent the wine there. If we go without drink today I shall take good care that it does not happen again.'

'Damn those fellows!' said lord Siegfried. 'It was arranged that they were to bring along seven panniers of spiced wine and mead for me. Since that proved impossible, we should have been placed nearer the Rhine.'

'You brave and noble knights,' said Hagen of Troneck, 'I know a cool spring nearby – do not be offended! – let us go there.' – A proposal which (as it turned out) was to bring many knights into jeopardy.

Siegfried was tormented by thirst and ordered the board to be removed all the sooner in his eagerness to go to that spring at the foot of the hills. And now the knights put their treacherous plot into execution.

Word was given for the game which Siegfried had killed to be conveyed back to Worms on waggons, and all who saw it gave him great credit for it.

Hagen of Troneck broke his faith with Siegfried most grievously, for as they were leaving to go to the spreading lime-tree he said: 'I have often been told that no one can keep up with Lady Kriemhild's lord when he cares to show his speed. I wish he would show it us now.'

'You can easily put it to the test by racing me to the brook,' replied gallant Siegfried of the Netherlands. 'Then those who see it shall declare the winner.'

'I accept your challenge,' said Hagen.

'Then I will lie down in the grass at your feet, as a handicap,' replied brave Siegfried, much to Gunther's satisfaction. 'And I will tell you what more I shall do. I will carry all my equipment with me, my spear and my shield and all my hunting clothes.' And he quickly strapped on his quiver and sword. The two men took off their outer clothing and stood there in their white vests. Then they ran through the clover like a pair of wild panthers. Siegfried appeared first at the brook.

Gunther's magnificent guest who excelled so many men in all things quickly unstrapped his sword, took off his quiver, and after leaning his great spear against a branch of the lime, stood beside the rushing brook. Then he laid down his shield near the flowing water, and although he was very thirsty he most courteously refrained from drinking until the King had drunk. Gunther thanked him very ill for this.

The stream was cool, sweet, and clear. Gunther stooped to its running waters and after drinking stood up and stepped aside. Siegfried in turn would have liked to do the same, but he paid for his good manners. For now Hagen carried Siegfried's sword and bow beyond his reach, ran back for the spear, and searched for the sign on the brave man's tunic. Then, as Siegfried bent over the brook and drank, Hagen hurled the spear at the cross, so that the hero's heart's blood leapt from the wound and splashed against Hagen's clothes. No warrior will ever do a darker deed. Leaving the spear fixed in Siegfried's heart, he fled in wild desperation, as he had never fled before from any man.

When lord Siegfried felt the great wound, maddened with rage he bounded back from the stream with the long shaft jutting from his heart. He was hoping to find either his bow or his sword, and, had he succeeded in doing so, Hagen would have had his pay. But finding no sword, the gravely wounded man had nothing but his shield. Snatching this from the bank he ran at Hagen, and King Gunther's vassal was unable to elude him. Siegfried was wounded to death, yet he struck so powerfully that he sent many precious stones whirling from the shield as it smashed to pieces. Gunther's noble guest would dearly have loved to avenge himself. Hagen fell reeling under the weight of the blow and the riverside echoed loudly. Had Siegfried had his sword in his hand it would have been the end of Hagen, so enraged was the wounded man, as indeed he had good cause to be.

The hero's face had lost its colour and he was no longer able to stand. His strength had ebbed away, for in the field of his bright countenance he now displayed Death's token. Soon many fair ladies would be weeping for him.

The lady Kriemhild's lord fell among the flowers, where you could see the blood surging from his wound. Then – and he had cause – he rebuked those who had plotted his foul murder. 'You vile cowards,' he said as he lay dying. 'What good has my service done me now that you have slain me? I was always loyal to you, but now I have paid for it. Alas, you have wronged your Kinsmen so that all who are born in days to come will be dishonoured by your deed. You have cooled your anger on me beyond all measure. You will be held in contempt and stand apart from all good warriors.'

The knights all ran to where he lay wounded to death. It was a sad day for many of them. Those who were at all loyal-hearted mourned for him, and this, as a gay and valiant knight, he had well deserved.

The King of Burgundy too lamented Siegfried's death.

'There is no need for the doer of the deed to weep when the damage is done,' said the dying man. 'He should be held up to scorn. It would have been better left undone.'

'I do not know what you are grieving for,' said Hagen fiercely. 'All our cares and sorrows are over and done with. We shall not find many who will dare oppose us now. I am glad I have put an end to his supremacy.'

'You may well exult,' said Siegfried. 'But had I known your murderous bent I should easily have guarded my life from you. I am sorry for none so much as my wife, the lady Kriemhild. May God have mercy on me for ever having got a son who in years to come will suffer the reproach that his kinsmen were murderers. If I had the strength I would have good reason to complain. But if you feel at all inclined to do a loyal deed for anyone, noble King,' continued the mortally wounded man, 'let me commend my dear sweetheart to your mercy. Let her profit from being your sister. By the virtue of all princes, stand by her loyally! No lady was ever more greatly wronged through her dear friend. As to my father and his vassals, they will have long to wait for me.'

The flowers everywhere were drenched with blood. Siegfried was at grips with Death, yet not for long, since Death's sword ever was too sharp. And now the warrior who had been so brave and gay could speak no more.

When those lords saw that the hero was dead they laid him on a shield that shone red with gold, and they plotted ways and means of concealing the fact that Hagen had done the deed. 'A disaster has befallen us,' many of them said. 'You must all hush it up and declare with one voice that Siegfried rode off hunting alone and was killed by robbers as he was passing through the forest.'

'I shall take him home,' said Hagen of Troneck. 'It is all one to me if the woman who made Brunhild so unhappy should come to know of it. It will trouble me very little, however much she weeps.'

17

How Siegfried was lamented and buried

They waited for nightfall and crossed over the Rhine. Warriors could never have hunted to worse effect, for the beast they slew was lamented by noble maidens, and many a good fighting-man had to pay for it in the end.

Now learn of a deed of overweening pride and grisly vengeance. Hagen ordered the corpse of Siegfried of Nibelungland to be carried in secret to Kriemhild's apartment and set down on the threshold, so that she should find him there before daybreak when she went out to matins, an office she never overslept.

They pealed the bells as usual at the minster, and lovely Kriemhild waked her many maids and asked for a light and her attire. A chamberlain answered – and came upon Siegfried's body. He saw him red with gore, his clothes all drenched with blood, but he did not recognize his lord. And now this man, from whom Kriemhild was soon to hear dread news, bore the light into her chamber, and as she was leaving with her ladies for the minster, the chamberlain said: 'Stay here! There is a knight lying outside the door – he has been slain!' and in the instant Kriemhild broke out into boundless lamentation. Before she had ascertained that it was her husband she was already thinking of Hagen's question how he might shelter Siegfried, and now she rued it with a vengeance! From the moment she learned of Siegfried's death she was the sworn enemy of her own happiness. Lovely, unhappy lady, she sank speechless to the ground and lay there for a while, wretched beyond all measure till, reviving from her swoon, she uttered a shriek that set the whole room echoing.

'What if it be some stranger?' asked her attendants.

'It is Siegfried, my dear husband,' she replied, the blood spurting from her mouth, such anguish did she feel. 'It was Brunhild who urged it, Hagen did the deed!' The lady asked them to lead her to the warrior and with her white hand she raised his splendid head. And red though it was with blood she immediately knew him as the hero of Nibelungland as he lay there, a most tragic sight. 'Alas, the wrong that has been done me!' cried the gracious Queen, in deepest sorrow. 'Your shield remains unhacked by any sword – you have been foully murdered! If I knew who had done this, I should never cease to plot his death.'

All her retinue joined their dear lady in cries and lamentations since they were deeply afflicted for the noble lord whom they had lost. Hagen had indeed taken a harsh vengeance for Brunhild's outraged feelings.

'You chamberlains must go and wake Siegfried's vassals with all speed,' said the wretched woman, 'and tell Siegmund, too, of my grief and ask him if he will help me to lament brave Siegfried.'

A messenger quickly ran to where Siegfried's warriors from Nibelungland lay sleeping, and robbed them of their happiness with his dreadful news, though they refused to believe it till they heard the women weeping. Then the messenger hastened to find King Siegmund, who lay unable to sleep (for I fancy his heart had divined his dear son's fate and that he would never see him alive again).

'Wake up, lord Siegmund! My lady Kriemhild has sent me to you. She has suffered a grievous wrong that afflicts her above all wrongs and she bids you help her lament it since it very much concerns you.'

Siegmund sat up. 'Of what wrong to the fair Kriemhild are you telling me?' he asked.

'I cannot withhold it from you,' said the messenger, in tears. 'Brave Siegfried of the Netherlands has been slain!'

'Do not mock people with such terrible news, saying that he has been slain, I beg you, for I could never cease to lament him till my dying day.'

'If you do not believe what I have told you, you yourself must hear how Kriemhild and all her suite are lamenting his death.'

At this, Siegmund gave a violent start, and, truly, there was cause. He leapt from his couch, followed by his hundred vassals – they snatched up their long sharp swords and in their misery made haste towards the wailing, when they were joined by a thousand of brave Siegfried's men. Hearing the women lamenting so dolefully it occurred to some that they ought to have their clothes on. – So great was the suffering embedded in their hearts that they had quite forgotten themselves.

When he came to Kriemhild, King Siegmund said to her: 'Alas for our journey to Burgundy! Who has robbed me of my son and you of your husband in this murderous fashion in the midst of such good friends?'

'Ah, if only I could discover who,' answered the noble woman. 'He would find no favour with me, but instead I should set such bitter things afoot as would give his friends something to weep for!'

Lord Siegmund clasped the noble prince to him and the laments of his friends mounted to such a pitch that the palace and the hall and indeed the whole city of Worms echoed mightily with their weeping. Siegfried's wife would not be consoled. They drew the clothes off his fair body, washed his wounds, and laid him on his bier, to the great harassment of his people.

'We shall always be ready to avenge him,' said Siegfried's warriors from Nibelungland. 'The guilty man is somewhere in the castle.' So saying, they all made haste to arm themselves, and returned with their shields eleven hundred strong, all of the excellent knights, under lord Siegmund's command. How dearly he wished to avenge his son's death, and small wonder!

They had no notion whom they should attack unless it were Gunther and his men, with whom Siegfried had ridden out hunting; but Kriemhild was far from pleased to see them under arms since despite her deep grief and great distress she was so afraid of her brothers' men slaying the Nibelungs that she forbade it; so with kind words she put them on their guard, as is the way among friends.

'My lord Siegmund,' said that sorrowful lady, 'what are you about to undertake? You have no idea how things stand. King Gunther has so many brave vassals that you are bent on suicide if you attack them.' Raising their swords aloft, they were athirst for battle; yet the noble Queen first begged, then bade those gallant warriors to refrain, and she was greatly troubled when they would not do so. 'Lord Siegmund,' she said, 'you must let the matter rest till you have a better opportunity. I shall always be ready to avenge my husband with you and if I ever obtain proof who took him from me I shall have the life out of him. There are many arrogant men here about the Rhine and they are thirty to one against you, so I should not advise you to start fighting. But may God let them prosper as they have deserved of us! Please stay here and mourn with me. As soon as it is daylight, you gallant knights, help me lay my dear husband in his coffin.'

'It shall be done,' they answered.

None could tell in full the extraordinary lamentation of those knights and ladies whose wailing was heard in the town, with the result that the worthy burgesses came hurrying along and added their laments to the guests', so distressed were they. Nobody had told them any reason why Siegfried had to die. Thus the wives of the good citizens were weeping there with the ladies.

Smiths were bidden to make haste and fashion a great, stout coffin of silver and gold and to furnish it with good steel braces. At which the thoughts of all grew very sad.

The night came to an end and they were told that it was dawning, whereupon the noble lady gave orders for lord Siegfried, her dearly beloved spouse, to be carried to the cathedral; and all who were his friends were seen weeping as they went with him. On their arrival at the minster many bells were tolled and the clergy were chanting on all sides. And now King Gunther and his men, and fierce Hagen, too, joined the mourners.

'Dearest sister, what sorrow is yours!' said Gunther. 'How I regret that we could not be spared this great bereavement! We must lament the death of Siegfried always.'

'You have no cause to do so,' said the wretched woman. 'If you regretted it, it would never have happened. I was far from your thoughts, I dare declare, when my dear husband and I were sundered from one another. Would to God it had befallen me!'

They vigorously denied their guilt on oath but Kriemhild cut them short. 'Let the man who says he is innocent prove it, let him go up to the bier in sight of all the people and we shall very soon see the truth of it!'

Now it is a great marvel and frequently happens today that whenever a blood-guilty murderer is seen beside the corpse the wounds begin to bleed. This is what happened now, and Hagen stood accused of the deed; for the wounds flowed anew as at the time of Siegfried's murder, so that those who were loudly wailing redoubled their cries of woe.

'I tell you he was killed by robbers,' asserted King Gunther. 'Hagen did not do it.'

'Those robbers are well known to me,' retorted Kriemhild. 'God grant that Siegfried's friends avenge it. Gunther and Hagen, it was you who did the deed!' Siegfried's warriors saw hopes of battle.

'Bear this sorrow with me,' Kriemhild told them.

And now her brother Gernot and young Giselher

arrived beside the bier and loyally mourned with the others. They wept for Kriemhild's husband from the bottom of their hearts. Mass was due to be sung and everywhere people were streaming towards the minster, man, woman, and child. Even those scarce touched by his loss began to weep for Siegfried.

'Sister,' said Gernot and Giselher, 'be consoled after your bereavement, as indeed you must. We mean to help you over it as long as we live.' But none was able to comfort her at all.

Siegfried's coffin was ready towards noon and he was lifted from the bier on which he had been lying: but the Queen would not yet let them bury him so that all were put to great trouble. They wound the body in a magnificent pall, and I fancy there was not one who was not weeping. Noble Uote lamented handsome Siegfried from the bottom of her heart, together with all her court.

When people heard the mass being sung and learnt that he had been laid in his coffin they brought countless offerings for the good of his soul, since he had no lack of friends as well as enemies.

'Let those who wish him well and who have friendly feelings towards me submit to grief and austerities for my sake,' said poor Kriemhild to her chamberlains. 'Share out his gold for the benefit of his soul.' And there was no child so small which, if it had reached years of understanding, was not asked to go and make its offering. And before Siegfried was interred more than a hundred masses were sung there that day. There was a great press of his friends; but when the chanting was over, the people went away.

'You must not leave it to me alone to keep watch over the illustrious warrior, at whose death all my happiness was humbled. I shall let my dear husband rest here for three days and nights, until I have looked my fill on him. What if the Lord should ordain that death should take me too? – Then poor Kriemhild's sorrows would be over.'

The townsfolk returned to their quarters, but she asked the priests and monks and all of Siegfried's followers to remain and keep vigil over the hero. Thus they had irksome nights and very arduous days, for many denied themselves meat and drink though they were told that those who wanted it could have food in plenty which Siegmund had provided. The Nibelungs subjected themselves to great hardship. During those three days, so we are told, those who were skilled at singing mass had to exert themselves greatly: but such a wealth of offerings was brought them that those who had been very indigent were now rich indeed. Poor people who had not the means were nevertheless told to go and make their offertory with gold from Siegfried's treasure-house. Since he was fated not to live, many thousand marks were bestowed for the good of his soul. Kriemhild distributed revenues in the lands around wherever there were convents and hospitals, to whose needy folk she gave ample clothes and silver, as a mark of the love she bore her husband.

On the third morning, at the hour of mass, the broad churchyard beside the minster was filled with the wailing of the Burgundians who were honouring him in death as a dear friend deserves. It has been reported that some thirty thousand marks or more were given to the poor for the good of his soul during those four days – but the life and great beauty of his body had come to naught.

When divine service had been sung many people were assailed by violent grief. Word was given to bear him from the minster to the grave, while those who missed him sorely wept and lamented. And so, with loud cries, people followed him away – not one of them was happy, man or woman. Before he was buried there were prayers and chants from the great concourse of clergy who were present at his funeral.

On her way to the graveside Siegfried's faithful Queen had been at grips with such grief that, time and time again, she had to be splashed with water from the stream. Her suffering was utterly beyond all measure and it is a marvel she survived it. She was assisted in her laments by many ladies.

'You men of Siegfried,' said the Queen, 'do me one favour, I beg you by your fealty. After all that I have suffered do me the small kindness of allowing me to gaze on his lovely head once more.' She entreated them so long in all the intensity of her grief that they had to break open his magnificent sarcophagus. Then the lady was led to where he lay and she raised his handsome head with her white hand and kissed the noble knight in death, while her bright eyes in their sorrow wept tears of blood.

The farewell was heartrending. They had to carry her from that place, for she was unable to walk – the splendid woman had fainted away. Lovely Kriemhild might well have died of grief.